"IT UNNERVES YOU WHEN I TOUCH YOU, DOESN'T it?" Joshua murmured, the knowledge rekindling his desire.

She shook her head.

"I mean more than you're used to," he went on. "More than you want to admit, even to yourself."

Victoria lifted her chin. "Joshua, I'm not a starry-eyed virgin."

Her skin was soft beneath his fingers as he straightened the collar of her jacket. "Then don't act like one. Love, I want the woman I see glimmers of. The one who trembles because she's afraid of shocking me. You're holding back. All the time. I'm tired of playing hide-and-seek, Victoria." His gaze roamed hungrily over her. "Try it. Try and shock me. . . ."

WHAT ARE *LOVESWEPT* ROMANCES?

They are stories of true romance and touching emotion. We believe those two very important ingredients are constants in our highly sensual and very believable stories in the LOVE-SWEPT line. Our goal is to give you, the reader, stories of consistently high quality that may sometimes make you laugh, sometimes make you cry, but are always fresh and creative and contain many delightful surprises within their pages.

Most romance fans read an enormous number of books. Those they truly love, they keep. Others may be traded with friends and soon forgotten. We hope that each LOVESWEPT romance will be a treasure—a "keeper." We will always try to publish

LOVE STORIES YOU'LL NEVER FORGET
BY AUTHORS YOU'LL ALWAYS REMEMBER

The Editors

MOUNTAIN MYSTIC

DEBRA DIXON

BANTAM BOOKS
NEW YORK · TORONTO · LONDON · SYDNEY · AUCKLAND

MOUNTAIN MYSTIC

A Bantam Book / September 1994

*If you would be interested in receiving protective vinyl covers for your
Loveswept books, please write to this address for information:*

> Loveswept
> Bantam Books
> P.O. Box 985
> Hicksville, NY 11802

ISBN 0-553-44431-X

Published simultaneously in the United States and Canada

To my sister, Lori Clark—
who found a family treasure
hidden in the mountains of East Tennessee
And to my grandfather, Byrd E. Daugherty—
newly found but much loved

A special thanks to:
Brenda Y. Smith, M.N., C.N.M., Associate
Professor, University of Tennessee–Memphis,
College of Nursing, for answering questions
and sending wonderfully concise and
informative literature. Her kindness and
generosity made my research a pleasure. Any
mistakes regarding midwifery practice and
procedure should be attributed strictly to the
author.

ONE

"It's the top-rated talk show! You can't say no."

"Yes, I can." Joshua Logan spoke evenly, but he gripped the phone tightly enough to turn his knuckles white. He had no intention of going anywhere in the near future. "You don't need me to sell the book. Five years ago, half the country bought *Touching History*. The new book will find its way without me."

Derrick Tremont, his agent, swore into the phone. "You can't still be serious about this 'back to the mountain' nonsense? I can understand your wanting to get off the university lecture circuit. You sure as hell don't need the money, and if you want to stop being an archaeologist and digging around in the dirt, that's up to you. You've already established your credentials. But you can't turn your back on this publicity tour!"

"I can, and I have. I thought we were clear on this, Derrick. My contract doesn't require me to put on a dog-and-pony show. As far as I'm concerned, the publisher bought the book. They bought the gimmick. They didn't buy me."

"For God's sake, you are the gimmick! A psychic Indiana Jones! What else would you call a flesh-and-blood scientist who admits that he can get psychic impressions from the ancient artifacts he handles?"

"Retired," Joshua told him flatly.

Silence stretched out through the miles of telephone cable. Finally, Derrick said, "I can't change your mind, can I?"

"No." *But I wish you could,* Joshua thought as he flipped off the mobile phone. A new mind would solve a lot of his problems. He'd let his psychic genie out of the bottle, and now he was having some trouble putting it back. He wanted out of the limelight, out of the high life, and back into real life.

When his head began a familiar throbbing, Joshua knew he wasn't going to get any more work done on the new cabin today. The past was closing in on him, and he needed space. Not bothering to pack up his tools, he headed for the most restful spot on the mountain. Once there, he leaned his back against a smooth tree trunk stained green by moss and slid slowly to the cool earth.

Welcoming the quiet of the familiar and primeval forest, he let the magic of his surroundings soothe his mind and make him whole again. When the relentless pounding in his head diminished to a faint, manageable touch of pain, Joshua opened his eyes to the lush green kaleidoscope of the Appalachian Mountains. He pulled clean air and the scent of morning dew into his lungs. Without a doubt, Joshua knew that coming back to live in East Tennessee had been the right decision.

He heard the muted whisper of water pulsing through the sluggish creek beside him, and he felt his equilibrium returning. The mountains had given him a place to fade away from the world, and more important, a place to let the echoes of the world fade away from him. Smiling, he realized this headache had been the first in weeks.

Soon the lush greenery would be replaced by the flames of autumn, his favorite season. Trading his career for peace of mind didn't seem like such a sacrifice when he got nature's beauty in the bargain. He'd come home, away from the emotional clutter of the cities, and he intended to stay. He doubted even an offer to excavate legendary Camelot would drag him off.

What was left of his career would have to come to him, and even then he wasn't sure he'd try again. Every time was like opening Pandora's box. Each new connection would only add to the emotions that had battered his consciousness for the past few years.

Emotions that didn't even belong to him. Sometimes, emotions so old they had to be measured in centuries.

Years earlier he made a mistake that both created and ultimately ended his brilliant career as an archaeologist. In his impatience to touch history, he had opened himself to the shimmer of emotion and knowledge that coursed through him as he held that freshly excavated artifact.

His abilities had created a maelstrom in the world of archaeology and academia. A profession that normally thrived on unexplained mysteries began asking questions he couldn't answer. All he understood was the seductive power of holding a piece of the past, discovering what had come before.

Touching History had been his attempt to explain. Instead of satisfying the curious, the book had catapulted him to celebrity status. After that, everyone wanted a piece of him, a bit of his soul. Everyone expected and wanted him to be just what Derrick said —a psychic Indiana Jones, archaeologist to the stars.

Joshua picked up a stone and sailed it past a small American chestnut tree. He made a sound that was partly sad and partly disgusted. How ironic, Joshua thought as he heaved himself up and began to walk. From the start, both the chestnut tree and his career had shown great promise, but then faltered.

Neither of them could handle the invasion. The chestnut couldn't handle the incurable blight that continued to kill American chestnuts. He couldn't handle the invasion of privacy or the emotional echoes that would surround him if he left the insulation of the mountains.

For him, there'd be no more cities, no more medical tests, no more psi tests, no more dog-and-pony shows. That much he could safely promise himself, he decided as he moved through the woods. The new cabin was almost finished, a testament to his conviction that he belonged there. He felt better than he had in years despite the fact he'd been driving himself to the point of exhaustion to finish the inside of the new house before winter.

"If you'd let the contractor finish it, you'd be living in there now!" he told himself as he ducked under the branch of a sugar maple. "You'd be sleeping there instead of in an old swaybacked cabin with a tin-patched roof that leaks like a—"

Abruptly, Joshua halted not only his words but his progress toward the gray, weathered cabin. A bright red splash of color drew his attention to the top of the hill. An ancient Range Rover perched on the side of the road as if its owner thought better of turning the truck onto the gravel driveway, which snaked down a steep incline.

Studying the old cabin, which nestled in a small hollow, Joshua noticed the door was slightly ajar. But then, he never bothered to lock it. For a split second he wanted to mentally reach for the echoes inside the cabin, to get a sense of who had invaded his house and why. Even as he suppressed the impulse, he swore silently, realizing that his abilities had become a habit, his way of staying one step ahead of the world. Until his return to the mountain, very little in life had surprised him.

And wasn't that one of the reasons you came home? To start living your own life instead of others'?

Joshua forced himself to judge the situation on evidence alone. He checked the truck and ruled out a flat tire. He also ruled out a neighborly visit. Folks on the mountain wouldn't put a foot in his cabin without an invitation. They stopped by occasionally, hollered at the edge of the porch, and waited for a response. If they didn't get one, they left.

Not a burglar either, he decided. Unless he was a very stupid one. He'd have to haul anything he stole up the hill to the truck fifty yards away.

The most likely explanation was some hiker wannabe with car trouble. He had a mobile phone at the new house, *if* the hiker wanted to take the twenty-minute hike over the ridge. But he hoped the stranger didn't. The only echoes in the new place were his own, and he wanted to keep it that way.

Joshua closed the distance to the old cabin. Wide steps of rough-hewn stone climbed to a covered porch, which was graced by two rocking chairs his grandmother had insisted he put there. *"J.J., no use havin' a porch if you don't sit on it! That'd just be a waste of trees."* She was right. These same rockers would eventually grace the porch of his new home, which was a much larger, stylized version of a traditional mountain cabin.

Quietly, he crossed the porch and with the tips of his fingers pushed the door. It drifted open until he could see the one-room interior. Nothing had been disturbed. Nothing looked out of place, not even the woman who was currently testing the comfort of his bed. Her eyes were closed as she allowed herself to sink gently back into the softness. Joshua wondered if she'd be disappointed to know that the Jacob's ladder quilt hid an overstuffed down-filled comforter instead of an old feather bed.

An aura of serenity, which had nothing to do with

psychic impressions, surrounded the woman as her arms spread out in a contented stretch. It was the sense of having made peace with herself and her life. Joshua envied her that peace and suspected some of her tranquility had rubbed off on him. Instead of angrily demanding to know why she had broken into his cabin, he made himself comfortable against the door-jamb.

From where he stood, he had a great view of his mystery guest. Black stretch leggings revealed every line, every curve of her legs until they disappeared beneath a long, brightly hued T-shirt of a coral reef and vivid fish, which undulated along the contours of her body. He liked the T-shirt and her legs, but doubted she'd be pleased to hear it. Instead, he quoted from an appropriate fairy tale.

" 'Well, well. Someone's been sleeping in my bed.' "

The woman lost her languid calm instantly. Arching her back in an unconsciously sensual movement, she came up off the bed with a sharp intake of breath. Her dark hair swirled as her gaze locked with his.

"And she's still here," he added, and raised an eyebrow.

Any other woman might have gulped, screamed in fear, stammered an apology, or gushed one in a rush of words; she did none of those things, although regret and apprehension did flicker across her expression briefly before disappearing. As her hair came to rest just below her shoulders, she settled herself, almost visibly drawing her poise about her like a mantle.

Joshua felt trapped in the serenity of her eyes, held hostage by the grace with which she faced him in what must have been an embarrassing situation for her. Even though he tried, he couldn't sense her emotions; she was closed to him. Deprived of his sixth sense, Joshua felt like he'd walked out of the sunlight and into the blackness of a cave.

For the first time in a long time he had to rely on intuition and physical cues to read a woman. Instinct told him this woman wasn't a hiker wannabe. Not with those sparkling white sneakers. She felt like country club and yachts. Then she introduced herself and blew away all his assumptions about the cool beauty in front of him.

"Hello. My name's Victoria. Victoria Bennett." Her voice sneaked inside him and tightened every muscle in his belly.

"Victoria," he repeated, more to buy himself time than anything else. Good God in heaven, what was a nice girl like her doing with a bedroom voice like that?

Nothing in her classically sculpted features hinted at the sultry power in her voice, which was earthy . . . quiet and smooth, liquid and hot. All at the same time. All of that with promises of more. It was the more that worried him. It was the more that would keep him awake that night.

"I've been looking for you," she said, and this time he caught the slight edge of nervousness in her voice.

"Next time give me a little notice. I'll sleep in and wait for you."

Pink tinged her cheeks, making him wonder how easily she blushed . . . and where. In the natural course of events, a man should know how easily a woman blushed before he knew what she looked like in his bed. With Victoria, he seemed to have done it backward.

He could still see the impression of her body in the bedding. When he lay down that night, he would wonder if her essence would sink into his bones the way her voice had, if he would feel her beneath him. The idea excited and disturbed him more than it should.

Instinctively he checked for a wedding ring and found none. That made him happy. Happy enough to forgive her for invading his cabin. *You've been living the life of a monk far too long,* Joshua warned himself, *if killer cheekbones are enough to make you forget about trespassing laws.*

As the awkward silence lengthened, Victoria racked her brain for a clever reason that would explain why she'd plunked herself down on his bed. Thinking clearly or cleverly was hampered by her unexpected reaction to the virile man before her. He fit her definition of a mountain man perfectly—tall, muscular, a face carved out of the past, eyes more blue than gray . . . mysterious, mystic almost.

Judging from the way the soft, well-worn chamois shirt molded itself to his upper body, he got plenty of fresh air and exercise. His shoulder dug into the jamb, and his hands circled his biceps. He looked like a man biding his time, probably waiting patiently for an explanation she didn't have.

"I'm sorry about . . ." She let her voice trail away as she moved toward him. The sudden narrowing of his eyes and the shake of his head warned her that the less said about how he'd found her, the better. Surprised, but perfectly willing to ignore the bed, she got to the point. "Dr. Grenwald sent me."

Joshua couldn't hold back a grin. "Remind me to thank him. I wasn't aware he was running a dating service."

"He isn't, so don't bother to thank him," she said dryly. "He's my backup physician. I'm the new midwife."

He laughed outright. "Miss Bennett, you've broken into the wrong house. I don't have a wife, much less a pregnant wife who might need your services."

"You are Joshua Logan?" When he nodded, she said, "Well, then you're the man I'm looking for. Dr. Grenwald seemed to think you might be willing to . . . help me."

"Deliver babies? I don't think so." He hadn't meant to sound so abrupt, but he knew what that delicate pause meant. He'd heard it too many times before. She wanted something important. Something she hesitated to ask. In his experience, when people hesitated, they usually wanted a piece of him.

Shoving off the door and stepping pointedly to one side, Joshua told her bluntly, "Looks like you wasted a trip."

Shocked by his abrupt change of manner, Victoria

stood rooted in place, wondering what she'd done to turn his attitude from amusement to anger. *Besides trespassing and then being rude enough to ask for a favor?* She was lucky he hadn't physically tossed her out before now.

She shouldn't have gone inside his cabin. Never mind the fact his door had been unlocked. Never mind that it swung open when she rapped her knuckles against it. She should have waited on the porch. *She should have . . .*

God, how she hated those words! Her life was filled with things she should have done. According to her parents, she should have: divorced Richard long before she did; asked for alimony; come home after the divorce and married someone suitable; or at least come home when they declined to lend her enough money to finish the midwifery program and get her master's degree.

She should have done lots of things. But she didn't. For once in her life she had listened to her heart. Otherwise she'd be wearing pearls and vegetating in Connecticut instead of delivering babies in rural Tennessee.

Refocusing on the present, Victoria tried to decide what to do. Logan was obviously waiting for her to say a polite good-bye and get out of his house, but she couldn't leave without at least trying to get his help, even if it created what her mother would call a "dreadful scene." Forcing her most contrite smile, she asked, "Would a completely sincere apology buy me any more time?"

"To do what?" Joshua asked, and ruthlessly quelled his libido, which produced an interesting list of activities—all starring Victoria Bennett.

"To plead my case."

He knew he should say no. That was the smart move. He even formed the word with his lips, but what came out was "Can you do it in twenty-five words or less?"

"I can try," she promised him.

The soft pleading in her smoky eyes was too much for Joshua. Against his better judgment, he hesitated, running a hand through his hair. If he agreed, she'd probably thrust an antique watch or piece of jewelry into his hands, hoping he'd do the psychic bit.

Joshua sighed. His psi ability didn't work like that. He couldn't flick it on and off like a light switch. Unfortunately, his curiosity about the lady had kicked in, aided and abetted by a healthy biological drive he'd ignored for too long. He wanted to see if he could read her possessions even if he couldn't read her.

"Look," she told him, "I'm not usually so rude that I wander into houses uninvited. I had no business coming inside. Please don't hold that against me. I truly am sorry."

"I'm not. Actually, you looked pretty good from where I was standing. Finding you in my bed was the highlight of my morning."

She blushed. "Then brighten up my day and give me five minutes, okay?"

What could possibly happen if he let her stay? Nothing, he told himself. Nothing at all if he remembered who she was and that she wanted Indiana Jones, not Joshua Logan. "All right. You've got five minutes."

Victoria resisted the urge to grin as she followed him the few steps to the old couch and armchair arranged cozily in front of the wood stove. For future reference, she filed away the fact that Joshua Logan was susceptible to puppy-dog eyes. With a hand motion he signaled her to take the couch and settled himself in the armchair.

His elbows rested on the arm supports, and his hands were clasped in front of his abdomen. She noticed a sexy gold ring on the little finger of his right hand. The ring's design looked old, old enough to be a family heirloom, and oddly familiar. Golden vines twined around each other, blending to form a circle.

To cover her overwhelming urge to reach out and touch Joshua's ring, she dragged her eyes back up to his face, which unfortunately was just as sexy, despite —or maybe because of—the intensity in his eyes. She had a soft spot for strong, silent types, and everything about him was strong—his mouth, his jawline, those big hands. Looking at him made her feel restless and excited inside.

Why now? she wondered. The fluttery feeling of attraction had been absent for so long, she'd forgotten what it felt like to have butterflies banging against her stomach. Why did she have them now, when it was the worst possible moment for the feeling to come back? She didn't need him, didn't need an inexplicable attraction scattering her thoughts and making it difficult to remember why she was alone with this man.

"So," Joshua prompted her, "show me what you've got."

"Excuse me?"

"I'm not a mind reader. It doesn't work like that." He held his hands cupped, palms up. "I have to hold it."

"Hold what?" Victoria asked, and cleared her throat. His hands were going to be her downfall if she couldn't keep her eyes off them. This fascination was so *juvenile*, but his hands and that ring struck a chord of memory, which was impossible. He wasn't the kind of man a woman could forget.

Joshua noticed for the first time that she didn't carry a purse. He clasped his hands together again. "Do you need to get something out of the truck?"

"N-no," she said warily, as if answering a trick question.

He leaned back in the chair and stared at her with surprise. She didn't have an antique trinket to press into his hands; she didn't even seem to know what he was talking about. In the space of several seconds he revised his opinion of Victoria Bennett. Maybe she didn't want a piece of his soul after all.

If she didn't want to use his abilities, then what did she want? Not being able to read her emotions fascinated him. With most people he could at least get a tiny hint. But not with her. "I think old Doc Grenwald is playing one of his little games. If he's let you come up here empty-handed, then he's sent you up here on a wild-goose chase."

"I'm not chasing wild geese," Victoria told him. "If you want to know the truth, I'm chasing you."

A rush of male satisfaction flooded Joshua, then slowly faded as he realized Victoria wasn't flirting. She was simply stating a fact in that damnable bedroom voice of hers.

"Thanks for the warning," he drawled, and moved forward to rest his forearms on his spread knees. Unexpectedly, his ego demanded that he ruffle her composure, make her acknowledge the chemistry he felt between them. "Saves me the trouble of having to chase you. What happens when you catch me?"

His tone was blatantly suggestive, sending sensual signals her body remembered all too well. There was no denying that she wanted to flirt right back, but she refused to give in to the impulse. She didn't have time for men; she needed to save her energy for the practice.

"When I catch you"—she told him matter-of-factly—"I intend to put you behind the wheel of that beat-up old Range Rover. I need a guide. Someone who knows all the back roads."

"Buy a map," Joshua snapped, stung that she appeared oblivious of the sexual undercurrents he was feeling.

"I have a map. What I need is a guide. Dr. Grenwald said you spent all summer roaming around and getting reacquainted. You grew up here, didn't you?"

"Yeah. I did."

"Great. I need to know this area backward and forward before winter drops a pile of snow and a sheet of ice all over it. What I wouldn't give for a nice flat, straight stretch of road." Regretfully, she shook her head. "Do you have any idea how confusing these mountain roads are?"

"You'll get used to it," Joshua told her curtly.

"I'll have to. I won't have much choice if you don't help me. Show me around the area. It won't take more than a couple of weeks."

"A couple of weeks!"

"I promise I'll work around your schedule, whatever it is. All I have to cover is the triangle of Mention, Bodewell, and Logan's Hollow."

"*All?*" Joshua raised his eyebrows. "That's a lot of territory, lady. You don't honestly expect to cover those three communities and everything in between? On a regular basis, I mean."

Victoria leaned forward. "Who else is going to do it?"

"Whoever did it before you got here."

"No one did it. That's *why* I'm here. Don't you ever read the newspaper?" she asked, wondering how he could have missed the front-page article in the area's weekly paper, *The Triangle*. "Those three communities paid for my education, and in exchange I agreed to set up a practice here. For at least three years."

"So tell them to hire you a guide. You don't need me."

Victoria gave a sigh and scooted back into the earth-tone sofa. "There's the rub. They paid for my education, and for as long as I practice here I get seven thousand dollars a year for living expenses. That's it. Everything else is up to me."

"Seven thousand a year won't even cover rent, utilities, and food," Joshua told her bluntly.

She shrugged. "Tell me about it! Rent and food are the least of my worries. I spent every dime of my savings on equipment, clinic space, supplies, malpractice insurance, and . . . you name it."

"That must have been some savings."

"Hardly. I also got a small business loan from the National Bank on the strength of last year's birth rate, Dr. Grenwald's recommendation as my backup physician, and my hospital privileges at Bodewell Hospital. The town and hospital have agreed to equip a small one-room ABC, but—"

"Whoa. You're talking to a man, and we don't know the secret maternity code words. What is an ABC?"

"Alternative birthing center."

Joshua motioned with his hand for her to keep going. "That's not terribly helpful."

"It's a low-intervention, family-oriented birthing facility. We can send the mother and baby home about twelve hours after delivery. Listen, Mr. Logan—"

"Call me Joshua."

"Joshua. What this all boils down to is that I don't have much cash. I need someone who can afford to go traipsing around the mountains for free. And"—she couldn't resist a quick glance around the clean but minimally furnished cabin—"Dr. Grenwald assured me that you were somewhat reclusive, but not hurting for money."

Laughing, Joshua thought about his last book advance and said, "Not exactly. This place is temporary. I'm building over the ridge."

Victoria's mouth formed a perfect *O*, and speculation lit her eyes a second before she smiled. "You mean that gorgeous cabin over the ridge is yours?"

Suddenly apprehensive, Joshua asked, "You've seen it?"

"I saw it this morning. I took a wrong turn about a quarter mile back on this thing you call a road. It's very . . . big," she said, although *humongous* would have been a better word. "Is all that space just for you, or did you invite the circus to winter with you?"

"I like space." Giving her a hard stare, he asked, "Did you go inside?"

"Well," Victoria began defensively, "that door was unlocked too and I was—"

"Looking for me," he finished, wondering what she'd touched and if he'd find her echo inside the place. "Is there a house within ten miles that you *haven't* been inside, looking for me?"

"I'm sorry. I didn't mean to . . . it's just that I really needed to talk to you. Where else am I going to get a guide for free?"

"Victoria, you don't need a guide. You need a keeper."

"Are you volunteering for the job?"

TWO

"Me?" Joshua asked, surprised. "Volunteering to be your keeper?"

"Well . . . I can respond to the idea of needing a keeper in one of two ways. If you're volunteering, I'll swallow my pride and ignore the insult because I need your help. If you aren't volunteering, I can afford to be insulted and tell you that I most certainly do not need a keeper. Especially one who goes around leaving all his doors unlocked."

"*Touché.*"

"I thought so," she agreed in a superior tone, but couldn't hide the amusement in her eyes. "I'm *so* glad you got the point. I wasn't quite sure you would." She sighed. "Chauvinist hides are thick."

A corner of Joshua's mouth turned up. He'd forgotten what it was like to have a long conversation with a woman who wasn't trying to impress him or worried about her mind being read. Not that he could read minds. He read emotions, not thoughts.

Except with Victoria he couldn't read anything. All he could feel was pure chemistry, a male attraction to a pair of incredible gray eyes. Intellectually he might like more insight into Victoria, but what he really wanted was to sink his fingers in her hair, which teased him by slipping demurely behind one shoulder and tumbling over the other.

"So . . ." Victoria prompted gently, "are you volunteering to help me or not?"

"You know, most of the women who break into my houses aren't nearly so pushy."

"Ah, well. There you go," she teased with a shrug. "I'm not most women."

"I think I'm beginning to figure that out for myself," he murmured, wondering how he could feel relaxed and hot at the same time. Wasn't he supposed to feel one way or the other? "Where exactly do you come from, Victoria Bennett?"

"Connecticut, darling. A veritable prison of privilege," she quipped, and then wished she hadn't when he raised one eyebrow in sudden interest.

"I see." Joshua congratulated himself on being right about her. She was country clubs and yachts. Or had been. Victoria was hiding secrets; he'd bet real money on it. She had a pair of emerald studs in her ears that probably cost more than a few months' rent, but she wore a Mickey Mouse watch with a black leather band.

Why was she living practically from hand to

mouth in the mountains of Tennessee? He tapped his index finger against the arm of the chair a couple of times, and then speculated, "My guess is that Victoria Bennett broke out of prison and ran off to become a midwife. Am I right?"

Not quite sure how to answer, Victoria busied herself removing an infinitesimal speck of lint from her leggings.

"Am I?" he pressed.

His question cut right to the heart of her feelings about Richard, her parents, and home. "Connecticut's not really like that." Victoria got up and walked a few steps toward the kitchen alcove. She made a pretense of inspecting the antique table's wood grain pattern. With her back to him she said lightly, "I was only joking, of course."

Like hell, Joshua thought. *If you were joking, you'd be looking me in the eye. What's wrong with Connecticut, Victoria?* He decided he wanted a chance to find out. "How long did you say this guide stuff was going to take?"

Victoria whipped around, wide-eyed, and then grinned. "The minute I saw you, I knew you'd do it."

"Don't jump the gun here. I haven't actually volunteered yet," he told her as he stood and began rolling up the sleeves of his shirt.

"Of course you have. Tennessee's the Volunteer State. I'm a damsel in distress. You have to say yes or risk your state's reputation."

"That nickname refers to fighting Indians and going to war. Showing a midwife around the Triangle doesn't compare. We wouldn't be risking life and limb."

"Obviously, you haven't seen a pregnant woman in transition." Victoria chuckled, thinking about the most intense forty-five minutes of labor. "Bloodthirsty Indians do not hold a candle. Trust me on this."

"I don't trust most people."

"How sad for you," she said quietly, and extended her hand as if to shake on their deal. "But not to worry, you can trust me. I'm not most people."

Joshua eyed the slender hand and blunt-cut nails. Normally, he didn't shake hands. The gesture was too intimate, almost emotional voyeurism, but he found himself in the unusual position of wanting to close his hand around hers. He wanted to know if the warmth in her voice was in her emotions too, and maybe he'd find out if he touched her. More than anything else, though, he wanted to touch her for the simple pleasure of making a physical connection.

When his palm slid against hers, the only sensation Joshua felt was the erotic friction of skin against skin. The only emotions he experienced were his own, and they tumbled together in an impossible mix of rationalization, intuition, and passion.

Victoria Bennett was just the kind of woman he made it a habit to avoid. He didn't need his sixth sense to tell him that. It was all there in her body language, on her face, in her glorious gray eyes, in her voice, in her career. She'd be calm in crisis, hot in bed, and the greatest shame of all was that maternal streak a mile wide. She was a midwife. The two went hand in hand.

He needed space, not nurturing. He needed to keep people out, not let them in. Unfortunately, she challenged him, made him forget all the promises he made to himself when he came back to the mountain. She made him forget everything except how her hand fit in his and how he wanted more than a handshake.

Staring at their hands, Victoria knew this was anything but a proper handshake. He wasn't supposed to be rubbing his thumb against the back of her hand. She wasn't supposed to feel tingly or shy. She wasn't supposed to be staring at the contrast of his tanned skin against the paleness of hers.

A handshake wasn't supposed to go on this long. Certainly not a business handshake. But this isn't business, she reminded herself. She'd known that the moment his hand found hers.

Silence stretched between them, so powerful it roared in her ears and stopped time. All she could focus on was the pad of his thumb stroking softly against her skin. She didn't dare look up, afraid of what Joshua would see in her eyes. He already knew about Connecticut; she didn't want him to see how much one silly handshake affected her.

Victoria Elizabeth Radcliff Bennett didn't lust after men in public. She much preferred to lust in her heart, where it was safe. Where she couldn't be rejected. Richard had taught her all about how important it was to hide emotions, about never letting anyone see what buttons to push.

Finally, she said, "I should go now."

Joshua heard her, but didn't release her hand. He

wasn't through memorizing the texture of her skin or the shape of her fingers. Softly, he asked, "Do you always do what you should?"

"I try to," she whispered, her attention riveted on his mouth now that she'd raised her head. Instinctively, she wet her lips, knowing that she wouldn't pull away if he kissed her. She hadn't been kissed in such a long time.

He dropped her hand and stepped closer until only a couple of inches of thin air separated them. "Maybe you should do what you *want* instead of what you *should*."

Swallowing, she asked, "What makes you think I don't do what I want?"

"Does anybody?"

She lifted her chin a notch, adjusting her line of sight so she could look into his eyes. "Do you?"

"Most of the time," he assured her without hesitation.

"But not all the time," she added softly.

"No, I don't always do what I want. Otherwise, I would have joined you on that bed, kissed you first, and asked questions later. As it is, I'm pretty sure I made the wrong choice."

"You did?" Her voice sounded flimsy and breathless even to her own ears.

"Love, I should have kissed you when I had the chance. Before I had time to think about it."

Victoria sucked in a small breath and couldn't help but compare him to Richard. Her ex-husband had always called her *Victoria*. Even in the throes of passion,

Richard managed to get all four syllables out. Hearing an endearment spoken in a husky male voice threw her off balance, tricked her into leaning a tiny fraction in his direction. Without really meaning to, she asked, "What's stopping you now?"

"An inconvenient sense of honor."

Several agonizing seconds passed as she realized he was turning her down. He had no intention of taking what she'd subtly offered, what she should have known better than to offer in the first place. Confused, she straightened, pink staining her cheeks again. "What's honor got to do with it?"

"Kissing you would be like shooting ducks in a barrel. Sort of like dueling with an unarmed man. Like—"

"I get your drift!" she interrupted angrily, dragging her fingers through her hair. When she'd collected herself a little more, she thumped him on the chest to move him out of her way. She needed room to pace.

Joshua couldn't have done a more effective job of bringing her to her senses if he'd dumped a bucket of cold spring water over her. After a several steps she turned around and put her hands on her hips. "Ducks in a barrel? Unarmed? Oh, please! Give me a little credit. I may have made a mistake peeking inside your cabin, but I am not the last starry-eyed virgin in America. I've been married. I'm a midwife, for God's sake. I probably know more about making love than you and five of your buddies."

Joshua clucked disappointedly. "I'm not talking

about making love, Vicky. I'm talking about chemistry. Lust. Sex. What do you know about those?"

She opened and closed her mouth several times, but nothing came out. She needed an exit line. She needed distance, and she needed both quickly. Backing away from him, she said, "I know enough to run as fast as I can when confronted with them. I don't need to be sidetracked. The only thing I have time for is building my practice. I absolutely don't have time to play games with you."

"Does that mean you won't be needing my services as a guide?" Joshua wanted to take the question back as soon as he saw her reaction. She stiffened, the healthy spark of anger went out of her eyes, and she composed herself in the blink of an eye. He felt her withdrawal in an almost physical way. She was once again the cool beauty he'd caught in his bed.

"You know I need you," she stated.

"You just don't plan on wanting me."

She glanced at the door and then at him. "Right."

"All you need is a tour guide"—Joshua walked to the door and opened it—"who keeps his chemistry to himself."

"Right."

"I think I can manage that." Casually, Joshua stretched his arm across the door, stopping her escape. "When do we start, boss?"

"I'll call you," Victoria said, deftly slipping beneath his arm and off the porch without a backward glance. "Dr. Grenwald's got your number."

Joshua watched Victoria climb the hill and murmured, "What a coincidence. I've got yours."

Victoria studied the colorful map on the table in front of her and gritted her teeth. She had to get her mind off the blatant challenge in Joshua's eyes and back on the task at hand. She was determined to have some sort of plan before she called Logan back. After the fiasco two days earlier, she wanted to be professional and organized the next time she saw him. She wanted to know at least *where* she wanted to go even if she didn't know the best way to get there.

The only trouble was, she didn't have the foggiest idea where the Mention and Logan's Hollow clinics were going to be. The towns were supposed to let her know as soon as each decided which school or church in their area could donate a day for her visits. Even worse, she didn't know where she was going to live. The weekly rates at Shepherd's Motel were going to skyrocket as soon as it got a little cooler and the leaves began to change color. Tourists would overrun the area for a brief time, trying to capture the event in photographs that could be only a pale imitation of the real thing.

The real thing. That phrase made her think of Joshua again. She could still see him vividly when she closed her eyes, brown hair touched by the sun, and big as all outdoors. Especially those hands. She hadn't been able to get them out of her mind. A memory of something flirted at the edge of her brain, but she couldn't pull it close enough to examine.

Exasperated with herself for wasting time, she threw down the pencil, which hadn't made one mark on the map, and tried to sort out her priorities. Instead of worrying about Joshua Logan, she should be out looking for a house. Pronto, in fact.

She heard the familiar clump of Wally Grenwald's footsteps in the entrance hall of the renovated old house that served as their offices. Wanting to catch him before he got out the door, she yelled instead of getting up. "Dr. Grenwald!"

Despite the fact that he was past seventy and looked every day of it, his voice boomed out strong and musical and got louder as he got closer to the back of the house. "You cannot get blood out of a turnip, dear. I have leased you three rooms at a rock-bottom price and given you every piece of spare equipment I have been able to beg, borrow, or steal."

"And I appreciate you more than you'll ever know!" Victoria started to yell, and then softened her voice when he appeared in the doorway of her leased clinic space.

Dr. Grenwald was a very rare bird among doctors; he didn't see midwives as a threat to his livelihood. Then again, he had always been more of a family practitioner than an ob-gyn. And, of course, he was planning to semi-retire when she got her practice established. In a way, his friendship could have been attributed to his own selfish motives. Regardless, she liked him.

"Doc, if I promise not to ask for anything, will you come in and see what I've done?"

"Helen's waiting dinner, but for you, I guess I could find a few minutes." He kept a poker face as he scanned her waiting room. Earlier, the freshly waxed wood floor had been obscured by a collection of old furniture and boxes. During the day, everything had miraculously found its proper place. Finally, he whistled in appreciation. "You whipped this place into shape in a hurry."

"Looks pretty good, doesn't it?" She couldn't keep the satisfaction out of her voice.

The Bodewell clinic was her home base, her pride and joy. The other two towns would be only makeshift clinics, but Bodewell was the center of her practice. Hanging her bachelor's and master's degree diplomas had been an emotional moment. Once it was done, there was no turning back; she'd officially hung up her shingle, so to speak. She had stared at the framed parchments and her midwifery certification for a long time.

She'd deliberately chosen to put them in the corner of the room above the round table she would use for counseling new patients. Around the rest of the room, wonderful illustrated posters and framed photos of the birthing process adorned the walls. The more graphic photos were in the examining room off to the left or tucked safely in her lesson notebook for the natural childbirth classes.

"Looks pretty good," Dr. Grenwald repeated, maneuvering his way through the maze of plastic crates filled with old toys. He passed over one of the three chairs grouped around the table in favor of the ratty sofa she'd disguised with a floral coverlet. "Different, but good."

Victoria hid a grin. Grenwald had a penchant for hospital-issue decor. If it wasn't shiny or plastic, he wouldn't have it. He liked his patients to know they were in a "professional" environment. She wanted her patients and their children to relax. One of the hardest challenges in rural areas was getting the women in for prenatal care.

Changing the subject, she said, "This morning I decided the exam room was too crowded for that wide cabinet I found over at McNamara's, so I stuck it in the cubbyhole that was going to be my office. Now it's a room for supplies and file cabinets."

"And where are you going to do your charts?" he demanded, looking over the rim of the half-glasses that were always perched on his nose. "You've got to have someplace to make your notes, talk on the phone. You'll wish you had that office."

"Aw, this table will be fine." Victoria patted the Formica-topped table and then gestured to the wall pocket files behind her, all neatly labeled as to the action to be taken once patient folders were slipped inside them. "I'll put a wall phone right here and get a long cord so I can go into the supply room if I absolutely have to have privacy. As for charts, I tend to scribble as I go—in the truck, in the exam room, wherever I have time."

Grenwald pulled at the short white hair along the back of his neck and heaved himself off the sofa. "Looks like you've thought of just about everything."

"Well, not quite. I haven't worked out my schedule, and I still haven't found a place to live."

He looked surprised. "I assumed you'd have that all settled by now. Joshua doesn't like having people around, but I didn't think he'd jack up the price to scare you off."

Used to the older man's non sequiturs, Victoria didn't bother asking for clarification. It was usually quicker to play along and figure it out for herself. "We didn't discuss money."

Laughing, Grenwald nodded. "Bet that took the wind out of his sails. Good strategy. Don't look too eager. That old cabin doesn't look like much, but all it really needs is a roof patch. You get that fixed, and it'll be just fine for the winter. I used to make house calls there when Joshua was only a little fellow, back before the family moved into Logan's Hollow. You're not going to be toasty warm in that house, mind you, but you'll be warm enough."

Click. As the doctor talked, the puzzle pieces slipped into place. Joshua was moving into that big showplace over the ridge, and he wouldn't need the cabin. Victoria looked down at the map in front of her. "Doc, could you show me exactly where the cabin is?"

After studying the squiggly lines for a moment, Grenwald poked a finger down on a spot. "Here. Or close enough anyway. When Joshua has the phone line brought into the new place, you could have service run over to the old cabin for next to nothing. Or you could use a mobile phone like he's been doing. The cabin's already got electricity."

In disbelief, Victoria swept her eyes from Bodewell down to Mention, across to Logan's Hollow, and back up to Bodewell. Joshua's cabin was right smack in the middle of the Triangle. She'd be able to get just about anywhere she needed to go in thirty minutes or so.

"Doc, how much do you think I ought to offer in rent?"

Twilight was beginning to color the sky by the time Victoria stopped her truck in front of Joshua's unlit cabin. Why couldn't the man be home at dinnertime like the rest of the world? She wanted to wrap up this deal before anyone else beat her to it.

The location was perfect. If Grenwald said the house was sound, then she was ready to sign a lease on the dotted line. As one of the few doctors in the area, he knew everything about the Triangle. He didn't always tell, but he knew.

Victoria banged a hand on the steering wheel. Just because Joshua wasn't there didn't mean she couldn't look around outside. No sense letting daylight go to waste, she thought as she opened the door of her truck. The yard was more weeds than grass, but she wouldn't have to worry about any of that until spring, when she put in the herb garden, assuming there was a suitable patch of ground.

As she passed the porch, she noticed the rocking chairs were gone, probably pulled inside for the winter. When she got around to the back, she saw a small addition jutting out and suspected it was the bathroom. Surprised, she realized the tarpaulin-covered object tucked beneath the roof overhang was actually a motorcycle.

Good grief, she thought. Who in their right mind would ride a motorcycle on these twisty roads? Surely not Joshua. He didn't look crazy, but she hadn't seen any sign of a car at either house.

Turning away from the cycle, she was overwhelmed by the sight of rhododendrons rising twenty feet into the air. Beyond the small backyard was an honest-to-God forest. Tulip trees towered more than four stories tall. She realized that trees just as big had probably been cut down with a two-man handsaw to clear out a space for the old cabin behind her.

She looked at the forest with something close to wonder. Soon the crisp nights would work their magic and set the deep green forest ablaze. She couldn't begin to imagine having a ringside seat for the show. Breathing in the clean air, she tested it for that brisk quality she associated with the arrival of fall. Not yet, she thought, but close. Real close.

"Impressed?"

Victoria screamed and jumped from where she'd been standing. Once she realized that it was Joshua who had spoken, she stilled her instinct to flee and sucked oxygen into her lungs in great gulps. Waving off his attempt to put a supporting arm around her, she rasped, "Good God! Don't you know better than to sneak up on people?"

"I hardly ever sneak up on people I've invited. They're expecting me and I'm expecting them. You see, that's how an invitation works. I invite you, and then we agree on a time."

So much for making an organized and professional impression, Victoria thought. Even in the dusk she could tell that he was quite happy with himself. She also noticed the well-worn jeans that were thin and molded to all the right places. The white T-shirt revealed muscle definition that the chamois shirt only suggested. He looked rugged and completely dangerous for her peace of mind. "I do have a good reason for being here."

"Sweetheart, that does not surprise me," he told her with a smile. "I'm just not too sure that we agree on what constitutes a good reason."

There it was again. An endearment. Highly inappropriate and completely unrehearsed. Richard had pushed all the emotional buttons deliberately; Joshua seemed to be doing it unconsciously. Richard reprimanded; Joshua teased. Richard never looked at her as if she were an oasis in the middle of a desert.

When her eyes suddenly looked away, Joshua realized his baser instincts were showing. She had that effect on him, and he'd have to help her get used to the idea. Either that, or spend a lot of time looking at the top of her head. A shy midwife was enough to boggle the mind and provoke testosterone.

Darkness and silence descended on the hollow at the same time. Clearing her throat, she asked, "Exactly what would pass muster as a good reason?"

"Did you bring me Chinese takeout as a gesture of friendship?"

"I didn't know I could get Chinese takeout around here. What other excuse will qualify?"

"Offering to help me move would be good."

"Right! That's exactly why I'm here." She rubbed her hands together and started past him for the front of the cabin. "I would love to help you move. I'm free right now, as a matter of fact."

"Victoria Bennett, that's a boldfaced lie." Joshua grabbed her shoulders and spun her around. "You don't expect me to swallow that tripe, do you?"

"But I am free right now." She laughed. "Promise."

"No, the other part," he told her as he squeezed her shoulders gently. "The part about coming up here to help me move."

"That part's . . . true too." She stumbled over the words as his fingers massaged her shoulders and his thumbs rubbed tiny magic circles against her collarbones, bared by the scoop neck of her top.

"Now, why would you want to help me move?" he asked, his eyes and hands promising pots of gold at the end of a sensual rainbow.

That thought sobered her instantly. She didn't believe in rainbows anymore. Richard taught her that it was foolish to believe in promises. Being lonely made her forget sometimes. Taking a step back, she told him the truth. "Because the sooner you move out, the sooner I can move in."

THREE

Joshua gave himself a few minutes to think before he said no. The prospect of having Victoria close was tempting, but he couldn't take the chance. He didn't need people around. He didn't need the responsibilities of being a landlord. He needed peace and quiet. How was he going to have that with this woman living practically in his backyard?

"No one's moving in here."

"Don't be silly. Why should a perfectly good cabin stand vacant?"

"Winter."

Victoria put her hands on her hips. "I'm going to have to deal with winter in the mountains regardless of where I live, Joshua."

"This cabin was built fifty years ago. It's hardly up to a winter."

"What's wrong with it?"

"Everything."

"Not according to Wally Grenwald. All this place needs is a roof patch and a telephone."

"Doc Grenwald doesn't know what he's talking about," Joshua told her, even though the doctor was right. The place might look a bit ragged, but it was sound. A few more pieces of corrugated tin would fix the roof problems.

"Oh, I think he does know what he's talking about. He said you didn't like having people around"— Joshua shot her a grim look—"and obviously he was right about that too. But I promise not to bother you. If you want to be an eccentric recluse, have at it. But first fix the roof and rent me the cabin."

Joshua didn't tell her that she bothered him already. A lot. Just standing there with her hands on her hips and her breasts outlined by the soft, clinging fabric of her blouse. She bothered him all right. "Why do you want to rent this place?" he asked. "Bodewell might not be up to par according to Connecticut standards, but the houses there have got to be better than my cabin."

"Bodewell isn't right smack in the middle of the Triangle."

"I know that."

"Think about it. As the crow flies, getting back and forth around the Triangle is easy. Except none of the roads is exactly a straight shot to anywhere. If I live in Bodewell, it'll take me at least an hour to get to my other clinics. I can live here and get anywhere in a half hour. Living here would be best."

"For whom?"

"For everyone."

"For everyone but me," Joshua corrected her. "I don't want neighbors, and I don't want to be a land-lord."

"You won't hear so much as a peep out of me. All you'd have to do is fix the roof. Surely, you were planning to do that anyway." She crossed her arms, daring him to dispute her logic. "You wouldn't just leave it like that and ruin the cabin."

No, he wouldn't, but that didn't make him like the idea of having a neighbor any better. Especially Victoria. He felt drawn to her. Living in this cabin, she'd be much too close, too accessible when he felt the need to talk. The whole idea of coming back to East Tennessee was to soak up solitude, not make new friends. Proximity usually led to companionship.

Sex he could handle. He wasn't so certain about friendship. He was tired of being disappointed in people, tired of being used by those he trusted.

"Victoria, you aren't going to like living here. It's too quiet for most people."

"I'm not most people," she reminded him.

"So you keep telling me." He rubbed the back of his neck. "You know there are cougars in this part of the country."

"Oh, please! I've already read all the travel brochures. There hasn't been a cougar even photographed in East Tennessee for something like fifty years. I doubt very seriously that I'm going to have to fight off big cats. Unless I buy one myself."

They stood for a few moments, sizing each other

up, weighing the possibilities. Finally, Joshua said, "You'll have to take the couch, armchairs, and the bed. I'm not moving them."

"Great. Then I won't have to buy furniture."

"You don't have any?" Joshua asked incredulously.

"No. I sold everything but the Range Rover before I came here," she told him, trying not to think of all the personal possessions she'd had to get rid of because she couldn't afford to move them or store them. She hadn't wanted to send them to Connecticut either. Her mother didn't like "junk."

Catching the wistful tone of her admission, Joshua asked, "Nothing like burning your bridges, is there?"

"It's an experience." Then she laughed. "Not to mention intensely motivating."

"I'll bet." Joshua took her elbow and led her toward the front of the cabin. "You'd better look inside again before you make up your mind."

"Oh, my mind is made up. Don't you worry about that."

Joshua stepped up on the porch and held the door open as she entered the cabin. "You may change your mind when I tell you how much the rent is."

"Ha! I knew this was coming. Grenwald warned me that you'd try to take advantage of me."

Looking at her back, Joshua raised an eyebrow and decided that old Doc Grenwald hadn't been far off the mark. He did want to take advantage of Victoria, but it had nothing to do with rent.

❖━━━━━━━━❖

About halfway to the old—to Victoria's cabin, Joshua decided walking had been a bad idea. It gave him too much time to think about her. He should have ridden the motorcycle; if he drove fast enough, he wasn't able to think about anything but the road.

Thinking about Victoria shouldn't have been a problem. She'd been true to her word about being a model tenant. She hadn't dropped by for a cup of sugar. She hadn't asked him to change so much as a fuse. She hadn't done anything to disrupt his peace. Except call him once to confirm that he could ride with her on Tuesday.

If she kept her word about not bothering him, why couldn't he stop thinking about her? Because she needed to be kissed. Because he doubted very much that Victoria Bennett would agree to a hot, satisfying, walk-away-when-it's-over affair. Because he didn't want a friend, and he had a gut feeling that Victoria needed one.

She'd moved in over the weekend, but she hadn't imposed on him to carry more than a few boxes, and then only because he hung around on moving day and insisted. He shook his head as he remembered unloading the truck. It hadn't taken long. The woman owned almost nothing.

Except her dreams, Joshua reminded himself, thinking of the excitement in her eyes when she talked about the beginning of her career, about looking forward to the first year of private practice. Maybe her dreams were all she needed. He hoped so; he doubted there would be much money to go with them. She'd never get rich being a midwife in East Tennessee.

As he walked through the woods and around the cabin, he could see her standing beside the old truck, intently studying a map spread out on the hood. She'd piled her hair on top of her head in what he assumed was an attempt to look more professional. Unfortunately, the closer he got, the less professional she looked.

Wisps of dark hair had escaped from the topknot and fluttered gracefully in the mild breeze, which molded the red, cotton-knit dress to her curves. From top to bottom the supple creation sported tiny red buttons that he knew would torture him all day, teasing him, daring him to flick them open. In short, she looked soft and kissable, and off limits now that she was a neighbor in need of a friend. He groaned in frustration, and Victoria looked up, concern filling her gray eyes and her expression.

"Are you all right?" she asked in a voice full of early-morning huskiness, but the sharpness in her eyes belied the sleepiness in her voice as her gaze ran over him.

Joshua realized that his groan had triggered not only Victoria's maternal instincts, but her medical training as well. He'd seen that look before as doctor after doctor tried to figure out what was wrong with him. When the doctors had finally and reluctantly given him a diagnosis, he hadn't troubled himself long enough to argue. Instead, he paid the bill and came home to Tennessee.

The constant headaches, the fatigue, and his inability to concentrate had all disappeared despite medical predictions to the contrary. Of course, he knew something they didn't. His problem wasn't a yuppie flu called chronic fatigue syndrome. His problem was the curse his mountain-bred grandmother called "the sight."

"I'm as right as I'm going to be," he answered.

Victoria narrowed her eyes at his evasive answer. The man didn't look sick or hurt. He looked healthy enough to wrestle one of Tennessee's black bears. His eyes were a cool, clear blue, and he had a way of looking at her that made her want to fuss with the fit of her clothes.

Resisting the temptation to button another button on her dress, she said, "Well then, good morning and thanks for helping."

He grinned, noticing the way her hand had strayed toward a button and jerked back. "Good morning. What's on the agenda?"

"I've got a list of about six patients from Dr. Grenwald. He says they came in once and then never came back. They don't live in town. They haven't responded to his office's phone follow-up, so . . . I'd like to track them down, make sure that they are in a regular prenatal care program of some kind."

"Sounds easy enough." Joshua joined her by the hood of the truck and pulled the map toward him. "Let me have a look at the list."

Victoria handed the list over. "Assuming we find them at home, I figure we'll need a half hour per visit, but I haven't the foggiest idea where we're going or how much travel time we'll need."

Joshua froze. He'd been thinking more in terms of Victoria introducing herself to the women, giving them a card, and urging them to call the clinic. "Visit?"

"Yeah." She turned a puzzled glance on him. "These women have some sort of problem, or they would have come back in. I've got to talk to them and find out what the problem is. Evaluate their cases."

The last thing Joshua wanted to do was to traipse in and out of the homes of pregnant women whose emotions were closer to the surface and screwed up by hormones. "Why don't we drive by, you knock on the door, and ask them to come into the clinic?"

Thinking she understood, Victoria laughed. "It's not an exam, Joshua. I want only to talk to the women. Face-to-face. It's harder to evade the issues that way or make promises they won't keep. We'll be talking about boring stuff like nutrition and prenatal vitamins. So you don't have to worry."

Not bothering to explain that his real reluctance was contact with *people*, Joshua told her candidly, "You do know that the most likely reason the women haven't come back in is that they don't have transportation or gas money. How are you going to fix that?"

"Home care maybe." She shrugged her shoulders. "The county health department warned me about the transportation problem. It's what made me decide to go after Dr. Grenwald's no-shows. The hospital won't back me if I do home deliveries, but I can do prenatal care in the home with no problem."

"No problem as long as they can pay you, or you can afford to work for free. If they don't have money for gas, they don't have money to pay you, Victoria, and mountain pride won't let them accept anything for free."

"Believe me, I'm cheaper than an ob-gyn. Besides, if money is keeping them from getting prenatal care, we can figure something out. A staggered payment schedule for the insurance deductible or something. They probably qualify for Medicare/Medicaid if they don't have insurance and have been unemployed for a while."

Surprised, Joshua stared at her. "Medicare pays?"

"Yep, for CNM's." At his blank expression, she elaborated. "Certified nurse midwives. If transportation's a problem, then we'll work out home visits. If insurance is a problem, we'll find out if they qualify for federal aid. And if they don't have transportation or health insurance, it's a sure bet that my phone call wouldn't have made any difference. Seeing is believing. I want an expectant mother to believe me when I tell her that she doesn't have to be ashamed of being poor and that she's not the only mother who's had to go on Medicare or Medicaid because she was having hard times."

Joshua looked dubious and glanced down at the list. "If I were you, I wouldn't look down your cultured Connecticut nose and tell these women that they're poor."

Victoria was appalled. "Give me a little credit. I wasn't going to say it like that!"

"Not intentionally, but it's the way you look, Victoria—like someone with all the answers. Like someone who doesn't have problems."

"But I'm barely making ends meet myself!"

"They don't know that. You don't present yourself that way. You've got emerald earrings, a Range Rover, and a killer red dress."

Victoria glanced down, stunned. "There isn't anything 'killer' about this dress. It would have been two years and ten pounds ago, but not now. A woman will know that, trust me." Meeting his gaze, she said, "The emerald earrings I got from my father for my sweet sixteen, and they're the only pair I own. The truck—such as it is—I got in the divorce. I live in the real world nowadays, just as they do. Don't worry, Joshua. I'll get my point across without insulting anyone."

"I hope so. You've got to meet these women on the level and part on the square," he cautioned.

She crossed her arms. "What's that supposed to mean?"

"They've had a belly full of people coming in to 'help' them over the years. You might have noticed the number of tiny missionary churches spread out in the mountains. A lot more than that tried and failed because they were too busy patting themselves on the back for being do-gooders."

"Are you telling me that these women might refuse my help because they're suspicious of my motives?"

"Yes, that's exactly what I'm telling you. By nature, we're a suspicious lot. Maybe it's the isolation. Maybe it's our Scotch-Irish ancestry. Maybe it's experience. Whatever the reason, we don't trust people, *outsiders*" —he amended—"to have our best interests at heart."

Victoria didn't miss the fact that he included himself in that group. "Grenwald said you lived away from here for years. That you traveled everywhere."

"I did."

"And you still think of people who weren't born on the mountain as outsiders?"

"Yeah, I do," Joshua told her, realizing that he'd never lost his identification with the place of his birth. As an archaeologist, he had spent years immersing himself in civilizations and cultures long gone. He'd lived in huge cities, college towns, and deserts. Yet he never once forgot he was born on a Tennessee mountain, or who he could count on should the need arise. "Old habits die hard. It's the way some of us were raised. Another generation or two and things will be different."

She shook her head as she recognized the problems she faced. "I don't think I can wait that long. If I don't try, the women who can't get to an ob-gyn will do what they've always done, which is ignore prenatal care and arrive at the hospital in the late stages of labor, totally unprepared and at higher risk for poor birth outcomes. That's if they get to the hospital at all. Home birth is legal in Tennessee. I don't see that I have any choice but at least to make the offer and let them decide how to manage their pregnancy and delivery. If they want to reject me because I have green rocks in my ears, so be it."

"You're dead set on this?" Joshua asked, knowing he couldn't refuse even though he wanted to. She made it sound too important. Made him believe it was too important.

"It's either that or sit around waiting for the mountain to come to Mohammed."

"Don't believe in miracles?" Joshua folded his arms across his chest and leaned a hip against the grille of the car.

"I don't believe in sitting around, waiting for someone else to change. People rarely do."

"That sounds like the voice of experience."

"It is. Are you ready?"

He resigned himself to a day of raw emotions rubbing against his consciousness. Maybe if he waited on the porch each time, it wouldn't be so bad. "Give me the keys."

"What for?"

"It's hard to start the truck without them."

"I'm driving," she said in a tone that clearly indicated he was foolish to suggest otherwise.

"You don't know where we're going."

"That's why I have you. I'll learn my way much better if I'm driving the truck."

"Correct me if I'm wrong," Joshua said, and held up an index finger to stop her from opening the driver's door, "but didn't you tell me that when you caught me, you were going to put me behind the wheel?"

"Figure of speech."

"Is this a gender thing? A statement about women being better drivers?"

"No, it's a captain-of-the-ship thing. It's my ship, and I get to steer."

"Ever heard of sharing?"

"I may have." She raised one eyebrow. "Isn't that where you get to play with my toys and I can't get mad when you break them?"

Joshua fought a grin. "How do you know I'll break anything?"

"I've seen you drive that sleek black motorcycle around curves that were not meant for sixty miles an hour." Victoria began folding the map. "What do they call the kind of motorcycle you have? A crotch rocket?"

"Yeah. Want a ride?" Joshua asked before he remembered his decision to limit his contact with her.

Victoria had already thought about living dangerously, about crawling up on the back of that machine, putting her arms around him, and holding on for dear life, flying around curves at speeds that would take her breath away. Assuming she had any left after getting that close to Joshua, her legs straddling his hips. But she wasn't about to admit any of that to Joshua. Her mouth went dry at the thought.

"No sense of adventure?" he teased as he headed for the passenger side.

"My sense of adventure is just fine." Victoria

opened her door in unison with him and slid behind the wheel. "It's my sense of impending doom that causes me to hesitate. You stick with that machine, and I'll stick with old Bessie here."

Not for the first time Joshua felt frustration at not being able to get a sense of her true emotions. Did she hate motorcycles, or was she scared of being that close to him? He wanted to know. He wanted to know if the thought of being wrapped around him on a motorcycle was as exciting to her as it was to him. The thought of her breasts pressed tightly against his back and her fingers roaming across his stomach, sliding lower, made his mouth dry.

He watched her, trying to find a clue in her expression or body language. She seemed to have dismissed the conversation and was pulling out a necklace from beneath her dress. A chuckle escaped Joshua as he realized it was more like a dog-tag chain than a necklace. Instead of tags, the silver chain sported Victoria's car key. Her jewelry selections continued to fascinate him: expensive earrings, Mickey Mouse watch, and car-key necklace.

"Don't laugh," Victoria informed him as she pulled the chain over her head. "It beats looking for my car key at three in the morning, when I absolutely have to get to the hospital."

"What about your house keys? Aren't you worried about losing them?"

"Of course not. I'm sure I could borrow an extra set from the landlord, or he could let me back inside the cabin." Victoria turned an innocent expression on him, her eyes full of mischief.

"I thought you said you weren't going to be any trouble."

"Have I been?"

"Not yet."

"Then let's cross that bridge when we come to it."

"Unfortunately, we'll be crossing several of those today."

Joshua was studying the list of names and addresses, but Victoria had a feeling that he wasn't talking about the incredible number of creeks that sliced through the mountains.

As she turned off the highways and onto the smaller paved roads, Victoria was amazed at the stark contrasts in the terrain. Unconsciously, her hand found its way to Joshua's knee time after time as she became excited about the scenery and wanted his attention. The roads had been literally cut into the mountainside. As often as not, sheer walls of rock rose on one side of the road, and a sickening drop lurked on the other.

The drops scared her as much as the escarpments awed her. The mountain fell away at the side of the road without so much as a guardrail in most places, and even the bushes beside the road were deceptive because they were really the tops of trees from below. She shuddered to think that a moment's distraction, especially at night or in the winter ice, would send the unfortunate motorist on a downhill ride that one had little chance of surviving. Forcing the depressing thought aside, she focused her attention on memorizing the area.

Mobile homes had been planted on every level spot available and had taken root, transformed into permanent homes with flower beds bordered with cinder blocks. She saw brick houses, tar-paper shacks, wooden houses marching side by side up the mountain. Many houses had been added on to over the years until they finally had enough rooms but no architectural unity. Other houses, hidden in little hollows beside the road, were no more than a rooftop peeking over the edge of the asphalt paving. Almost all the wooden houses had a porch enclosed with a picket-fence railing.

Some of the towns they passed through were only wide spots in the road—a collection of buildings around a stop sign or railroad tracks. Victoria couldn't imagine living less than twenty feet from an active train route, and wondered why the houses hadn't shaken apart over the years. A few dead coal mines also dotted the landscape, their chutes and works rusted with age and idleness. The mines looked like ugly tentacled creatures hunkered down in the midst of a gorgeous panorama.

The leaves were beginning to turn color, but foliage still sheltered much of the road from sunlight. Patches of light dappled the shade as she negotiated the serpentine road and hairpin curves that would have nauseated her if she hadn't been driving.

"Slow down," Joshua advised.

"But I'm only doing thirty!"

"The road drops out from under you around the next curve."

"Oh."

She glued her eyes on the road where it disappeared around the mountain, and Joshua kept his eyes on her, noticing the way her hands clutched the steering wheel. "Nervous?"

"About what?"

"About your first patient."

"Oh. No, I've had lots of patients. It's the road and all that talk about it dropping out from under me. Why don't you people have guardrails?"

"We do. In some places."

Victoria shot him a sour look. "Not in enough places."

Ignoring her displeasure, Joshua asked, "How can you have had a lot of patients? This is your first practice."

"I'm new but not untried, for heaven's sake. I've done more clinical course work than I care to remember. They don't give us a book exam and turn us loose on the unsuspecting public!"

"Well, what do they do? I mean, you can't exactly call up Acme Midwife School."

"Actually you can. There are about forty nurse-midwifery programs, but my bachelor of fine arts degree didn't qualify me. So I went to nursing school to get my R.N., much to the horror of Richard, my ex-husband. After the divorce I got my midwifery certification and a master's degree from Columbia University."

"Why'd your husband object to nursing school?" Joshua asked as he pointed out another sharp curve.

With her attention split between the road and the conversation, she answered the question more honestly than she intended. "Wives don't work; they dress well, volunteer, and entertain. A really good wife can do all three simultaneously."

"I take it that wasn't enough for you."

Victoria hesitated. The truth was that Richard wanted a business arrangement with bedroom privileges, not a real marriage. Unfortunately, he hadn't let her in on the secret until he slipped the ring on her finger and announced his agenda for success, expecting her to fall in line like the well-connected society debutante he'd thought he'd married.

Instead of telling Joshua the truth, she gave him the same flip, easy explanation that satisfied most people. "Midwifery beats wallpapering hands down as the acid test for a relationship."

"But you weren't a midwife when you were married to Richard," Joshua objected astutely. "You didn't get into the midwifery program until after the divorce."

Abruptly, she asked, "How much farther?"

Joshua's eyebrows shot up. He got the message loud and clear. Victoria's failed marriage was not open for discussion. Fair enough. He didn't want to have to drag all the details of his past into this relationship either. *Relationship?* He thought he'd settled that question this morning. *Then why are you nosing around in her past?* Because I never could resist nosing around in the past, he admitted honestly.

"How much farther?" she asked again.

"Not very far. A couple of miles up the road you'll see a creek and a railroad trestle. Chapel Road is on your left. After that I don't know how far it is. We'll have to start checking the mailboxes."

"What mailboxes?" Victoria asked. "We haven't seen one in"—she broke off and looked back over her shoulder for a second—"there it is again!"

"What?" Joshua craned his head around to survey the view from the back window.

"The yellow signs with the black arrows that point out the turns and curves. They all have holes in them like they've been victimized by big metal-eating moths. At first I thought it was my imagination, but it's not. There are holes in every single one of them." She pointed. "There! Another one."

"Oh. That."

"Oh. That," she mimicked impatiently. "Don't you think it's a little weird?"

"No, but then, I grew up here." Joshua shifted uncomfortably as he confessed, "I put my share of holes in these signs. Actually not in these *particular* signs, as I recall."

An uneasy suspicion began to take root in Victoria's mind. "Joshua, how did you put holes in signs?"

"With a gun," he answered bluntly. "We shot them from moving cars for target practice."

If she hadn't been driving, Victoria would have

gaped at him. Instead, she gaped at the road. "You shot poor, defenseless road signs for fun?"

"Well, not anymore."

"But you did."

"I did." Not that he was thrilled to admit it. "Obviously, someone else still does."

"Why?" she asked incredulously. The whole concept was like a foreign language to Victoria—incomprehensible. "From a car no less! On roads like this!"

"Guns and mountain men go together. We were the original survivalists. In Texas they play cowboys and Indians. In Tennessee we play moonshiners and revenuers."

"I don't believe that for a minute. Why did *you* do it? You don't look like—"

"Like I could be young and stupid and drunk and angry? Well, I was angry a lot when I was younger. I was angry until I got off the mountain."

"Why'd you come back?" Victoria asked quietly.

"I don't like crowds. Turn here."

Automatically, Victoria slowed the truck and flipped the blinker, but she came to a complete stop before she turned. Victoria pursed her lips and looked at the bumpy, twisted gravel road. "Are you serious? You call that a road?"

"If you're worried about the truck, maybe we should go home and phone the woman," Joshua suggested hopefully. "No sense overheating the engine in this old thing."

Grinning, Victoria said, "You're not going to discourage me, Joshua. I'll climb a lot bigger hills than this one if that's what it takes to get what I want."

"And what is that?" he asked.

"A life," Victoria told him as she punched the gas pedal and drove the truck onto what bore more resemblance to a washboard than a road. "Which patient is this?"

"Naomi Marlowe."

"Pretty name. There is a Marlowe's Wash-O-Rama in Bodewell. Is she related?"

"Yes and no."

"Well, which is it?"

"Naomi's one of the Mention Marlowes. They don't speak to the Bodewell Marlowes, but they are definitely related if you take the family tree back to about 1860, when the feud started."

"How do you know all of this?"

"My grandmother is something of an authority on the bloodlines and family feuds in this area."

"In this day and age you expect me to believe that there is still a family feud that has been going on since the Civil War?"

"On the mountain we don't forget. We don't forgive. You betray us once. You might betray us again."

"That's a little harsh, Joshua."

"Folks who settled this area were hard people, Victoria. They had to be. They were nonconformists; they didn't fit in or want to try. Many of them had been run out of work by slavery, which took all the jobs for an honest hardworking man in the flatlands. East Tennessee was overwhelmingly Union."

"Tennessee's a Southern state! They joined the Confederacy."

Joshua shrugged. "They were the last to secede and the first to be readmitted. One county furnished more federal soldiers than it had voters. To make a long story short, the Mention Marlowes sided with the Union, and the Bodewell Marlowes are descended from the brother who fought for the South."

"You're kidding, right?"

"Dead serious . . . even though no one's killed anyone since about 1936, when Harlan Marlowe shot James Marlowe in a driveway dispute. Ah, here we are!"

By the time she came to the end of a narrow dirt driveway and found the house which was hidden by a screen of trees, Victoria still hadn't decided if he was teasing her. Bracing herself, Victoria murmured, "This doesn't look so bad."

Clothes hung limply on a line stretched between two wooden posts. The barren brown rows of a played-out garden were a small distance away from the clothes, and a shed nearby looked ready to fall over at the gentle push of one finger. Both the shed and the house were sided with roof shingles.

Victoria killed the engine and took a deep breath. "Okay, let's go."

"You go. I'll wait out here and catch twenty winks."

Turning on him, Victoria ordered, "Think again, Joshua Logan. You just spent close to half an hour convincing me that these women are going to be suspicious of me no matter what I do. You were born on the mountain, and that ought to count for something. So you get out of this truck and come with me. Having you along might even get my foot in the door."

When he hesitated, Victoria noticed the dread in his expression. What on earth did he have to be apprehensive about? "Joshua, it's just a visit. Help me do what I came to Tennessee to do. These women need me, or someone like me." She touched his arm, gently resting her hand until he could feel the weight of it. "And I need this practice. It's all I have."

"I'll knock," he finally agreed, wishing he hadn't helped her unload her damn truck when she moved in. Regardless of where she grew up or came from, he knew she was telling the truth about the practice. He pulled the door handle and got out. Resting a forearm against the roof of the truck, he leaned back in and told her bluntly, "But I don't shake hands, and I wait on the porch. Understood?"

Stunned, Victoria realized that Joshua was serious. This wasn't simply a male aversion to being stuck in a room full of baby talk. Something about these visits spooked him. Genuinely spooked him. Grateful for his help under the circumstances, Victoria smiled and said, "All right. Let me get my things."

Quickly, Victoria got out and retrieved her medical bag and Naomi's file from the cardboard box on the backseat. By the time she returned her attention to Joshua, he stood at the edge of the porch, hands on his hips.

"Hello!" he shouted, and when the front door opened he climbed the steps.

Victoria walked up beside him, surprised at the tension she could feel in the air. She wondered if it was coming from the woman or from Joshua. Calmly, she caught and held the wary gaze of the blonde behind the screen door as she asked, "Naomi Marlowe?"

"What do you want? I haven't got the money to buy anything."

"Only a flatlander fool would come hell and gone up this mountain to sell you somethin'," he told her.

Victoria's eyes widened at Joshua's curt response and the subtle change in his speech. His voice had always been rich and strong, but now had an edge to it that proclaimed him a native son. The woman they'd come to see noticed it too and gave the duo on the porch a little more respect when he made introductions.

"I'm Joshua Logan, and this is Victoria Bennett. She's an associate of Dr. Grenwald's."

"I paid my bill," Naomi told them, and started to close the wooden door.

"It's not about that, Naomi," Victoria told her quickly. The door stopped closing, and Joshua listened as she continued in a warm, natural way that was full of confidence, yet reassuring and nonthreatening. "Dr. Grenwald has asked me to complete the files on some of his patients. I'm a midwife. I wondered if we could talk for a few minutes?"

"Midwife?" Naomi asked, straightening a little and opening the door wider.

Joshua mentally tipped his hat to Victoria. She'd managed to melt the iceberg a tiny bit. He waited to see how far she could get.

"Yes. I'm opening a practice in this area, and Dr. Grenwald is my backup physician."

"Bodewell's a long way."

"Just my main clinic is in Bodewell. I'll be seeing patients in Mention on Tuesdays. I handle deliveries at Bodewell Hospital."

"My heart's set on havin' this baby at home. That's what Ma did," Naomi said as her sharp eyes moved over Victoria, noting the medical bag. "I'd feel a heap better if I had a granny with me."

Knowing the term "granny" was synonymous with midwife to the people in the community, Victoria explained, "I'm sorry, but I can't attend home deliveries."

Naomi's face fell.

Victoria continued gently. "The hospital won't support my practice if I do." Victoria broke off as if just remembering something. "They did agree to dedicate one room for an alternative birthing center, which is more like a home setting, if that's what you're interested in. Mother and baby can usually go home in about twelve hours. It's cheaper too."

Perking up, Naomi asked, "How much less?"

"Maybe I could come in? I could answer your questions about the ABC room at the hospital, and you could help me complete this file."

When Naomi agreed, Victoria explained that Joshua didn't want to offend, but he really needed to stretch his legs. Would Naomi mind if he waited outside? Shortly, Joshua was left standing on the porch, exactly where he wanted to be. He breathed a sigh of relief. If the other visits went as smoothly, he might actually get home without picking up any more emotional echoes for his collection.

Lately, the only emotions he was interested in were Victoria's, and she kept them hidden, where he couldn't touch them. He knew as much about her as any Joe off the street. She'd been through a bad divorce, and she wanted a life of her own, separate from her past.

Absently, he rubbed his arm where her hand had rested, and wondered what to do about Victoria.

"Not a bad day's work," Victoria told him as she pulled up alongside his house. "I think four of the six are going to come into the clinic next Tuesday. Thanks for the help."

"You're welcome." Joshua forced himself to get out of the truck without asking Victoria for a date. All day the thought had been on his mind. Ever since she came out of Naomi's house, eyes shining and wearing a smile that would have lit up New York.

He wasn't sure he'd be able to take many more days like this one—cooped up in the truck with her fragrance hammering away at his resolve. She smelled like cinnamon and spice. And sex, if he told the God's truth. He couldn't explain it, but his attraction to Victoria went way beyond incredible perfume.

When the other truck door slammed behind him and he heard Victoria's footsteps, he closed his eyes. Hadn't he suffered enough today? The woman had touched him every three seconds, asking for or lending support, inviting him to share a joke, pointing out a clump of wildflowers that refused to give in to the change of seasons. None of those touches had been remotely sexual, and every one of them had made him intensely aware of her as a woman.

"May I come in and borrow your phone? I won't have one until next week, and I wanted to check the messages at my office."

"Since when have you needed an invitation to come inside?" asked Joshua, resigned to the inevitable.

"Since you made such a fuss last time!" Victoria told him. "Besides, you weren't living here then."

"What difference does that make?" Joshua made a sound that was clearly intended as a snort of disbelief, and he unlocked the door. "You waltzed into the old cabin too, and I was living there then as I recall."

Victoria ignored his remark, knowing he was right. "May I borrow the phone or not?"

Sometime within the next fifteen minutes he was going to kiss her, and to hell with whether or not it was a good idea.

FOUR

Pushing open the door with one hand, Joshua reached out and straightened the collar of her dress with the other, his thumb brushing against soft, warm skin exactly as he planned. The moment was electric. Joshua was fascinated by the differences between them, the contrast of dark and light. He'd definitely been celibate for too long.

"You can borrow anything you want," he said. Slowly dropping his hand, he added, "Except the bed, although I might be willing to share."

Victoria felt the heat of a blush roar through her. All day he'd been friendly but withdrawn, as if he were keeping himself separate from the world around him. Now his eyes met hers, and he held her gaze, creating a wordless intimacy. Suddenly the butterflies in her stomach woke up and started a frantic pounding against her rib cage, drumming a sensual red alert along all her nerve endings. With one look he'd cut through the polite, professional demeanor she'd managed to maintain. With one touch he'd cut through her efforts to forge a harmless friendship.

She probably had a better chance of holding back the sunrise than keeping thoughts of being kissed from her face, because that's all she could think about. An engraved invitation couldn't have been more plain than the way her tongue darted out along the edge of her lips, and yet he waited, letting the silence between them build a tension that threatened to snap at any moment.

Nervously, she lowered her eyes, but got only as far as his mouth. She swallowed. Why did the man have to be so big, so gorgeous, so slow to take what he wanted? What was it about him that made it so difficult for her to hide her attraction? She'd had years of practice at pretending to be indifferent to sexual attraction, of convincing herself that she was better off alone. Now she blushed and her nipples got hard because a man stared at her with lust in his eyes.

Then why doesn't he do something about it? A certainty in Joshua's expression convinced her that it was only a matter of time. *He enjoys the waiting, the tension. He likes to tease.* Victoria began to worry, not about if he was going to kiss her, but whether or not she could outlast him.

Starting anything with Joshua would be a mistake, she told herself firmly. She was so close to getting her life neatly arranged. She'd finally stopped wanting to be held in someone's arms at night. She couldn't let her emotions get all tangled up again. Especially not in a relationship with a man who could affect her like this before he ever touched her.

Faintly, she heard herself say, "We should go in."

"Yeah. We should," Joshua echoed as he backed into the house and reached for her hand to draw her after him. If they went in, maybe he could avoid the inevitable, maybe he could get through the day unscathed. He managed to ignore the way the red dress shifted and flowed over her curves as she passed him, but the disappointed look on her face did him in. "Ah, what the hell!"

Victoria got only a glimpse of a big mahogany-colored couch, hardwood floors, watercolor paintings of Plains Indians, and lots of open space before Joshua kicked the door shut and pulled her hard against him, letting go of her hand as if he were certain she'd stay in his arms of her own volition. He murmured, "This morning I promised myself I wasn't going to do this."

Then his lips came down on hers, giving her what she'd wanted since that first day in the cabin. He was tall and hard, drawing her up against the wall of his chest. Everything about him was deliberate, from the way he nibbled at her lips to the way he adjusted his body to cradle hers. As if he'd been thinking about this kiss for a long time.

Victoria melted into the sensation of being savored. She put common sense on hold and forgot everything but the feel of muscle beneath her fingers as they crept up his chest and around his neck. Three years was a long time to wait to be kissed again.

For Joshua, the contact of their lips had signaled

the point of no return. Her mouth was soft and yielding beneath his, allowing him to take his time. At the touch of his tongue against the seam of her lips she opened her mouth slightly. With no more invitation than that, he swept his tongue into the moist, welcoming warmth.

Everything about the kiss was an exploration, because he didn't know what she was feeling. He didn't have a window into her emotions to tell him what she wanted. All he had to guide him was the physical response of her body to his, the way her tongue twined with his, the way a tiny movement of her hips urged him silently onward. When Joshua realized his hand was straying to the first of the buttons that had driven him crazy all day, he finally broke the kiss.

Joshua touched his forehead to hers and allowed himself to catch his breath. Kissing Victoria was like running a marathon, and he needed his second wind. So did she, because she drew in a extended breath and exhaled slowly. Long, pregnant seconds passed as neither of them moved. Joshua finally cleared his throat and stepped back.

With tiny movements Victoria squared her shoulders and smoothed her dress. As incredible as that kiss was, she knew better than to let a man know he had the power to shake her right down to her toes. What was that television commercial? Never let them see you sweat. Silently she added—or need, or want.

When she felt she could trust her voice not to come out in a rasp, she said, "I guess we had to . . . to get that out of our systems."

"You don't honestly think we got it out of our systems?" Joshua asked with a scowl. "I know it's not out of mine. The question is, what are we going to do about it?"

"Nothing."

"We tried that. It didn't work."

"Why do we have to do anything? Can't we chalk it up to curiosity and forget it? It's over and done with. We can go back to being friends."

"Or we can go forward to being more than friends."

"That's not a good idea." Victoria shook her head vigorously, causing the tendrils around her face to brush against her jaw.

"Neither is letting the tension between us get so thick you could cut it with a knife. I'm afraid that what we've got here, love, is an ongoing chemistry experiment."

"Which is more than likely going to blow up in our faces if we don't get smart. You're busy being retired from whatever it was that you did, and I have a practice to run. Let it go, Joshua."

"Not 'it,'" Joshua corrected her softly. "*You*. Let *you* go. That's what you'd really like. Then you wouldn't have to worry."

"About what?"

"About me. Takes two to tango, Vicky. You're afraid that if I lead, you'll follow."

"That is ridiculous macho double-talk. The only thing I'm afraid of is being sidetracked when I need to be concentrating on my patients."

"I don't think so." Joshua refreshed her memory. "Tell me you didn't want me to kiss you in the cabin the first day we met. Tell me you weren't disappointed tonight when I let the moment on the porch slide by without doing anything. Tell me you didn't want that kiss every bit as much as I did." When she opened her mouth to deny it, he cautioned her, "Be honest, Victoria."

She pressed her lips together. Taking a deep breath, she admitted, "I'm as curious as the next person."

"Curious? *Curious* is a little weak, Vicky. I think we both knew it was inevitable. The only question was how long we could hold out."

"We?" Victoria raised her eyebrows and her voice. "I was holding out just fine. You were the one who couldn't hold out."

"Was that your idea of holding out?" Joshua retorted.

"Your male ego is obviously embellishing what happened between us."

"My imagination's pretty good, but it's not good enough to imagine that sexy little hip push you did when you were belly to belly with me."

For the second time since he'd known her, Joshua watched Victoria go quiet as the spark of anger vanished from her gray eyes; he watched her pull all the emotions off her face and tuck them back inside, where they belonged, although the faint stain of a blush remained. He was beginning to recognize her emotional control as a defense. Whenever the discussion got too heated, whenever too much was at stake, she got quiet; she got control.

Victoria brushed past him, intending to leave. "If you're still helping me, I need to go to the area around Logan's Hollow on Thursday. I'll have some more names to follow up."

"What about the phone?" Joshua asked casually as she swept over the threshold in a dignified retreat. "I thought you wanted to call your office for messages."

Instantly, she stopped, and cursed under her breath. When she didn't say anything else, he guessed she was trying to decide how badly she wanted to check her messages. Must have been pretty badly, because she turned around.

"I'd rather not wait until tomorrow to check the machine. I don't have patients yet technically, but the hospital might have called."

"Then come in. Just don't expect me to ignore temptation should opportunity present itself."

"It won't present itself," Victoria promised with a confidence she didn't feel.

"Give me a minute. I'll arrange something."

Exasperated, Victoria walked back into the house. "Don't bother. I'm not in the market for a . . . relationship."

"Who said anything about a relationship?" he asked, and walked back into the living room.

Fuming, Victoria followed him. "Wake up, Joshua. You might be hiding out from the world up here, but even you should know these are the nineties. Free love has been replaced by safe sex. Monogamy is in; casual sex is out."

Chuckling, Joshua grabbed the phone from a shelf on a wall-to-wall bookcase which was filled with carved stone bowls and pottery cups that were artfully arranged. He held the phone out to her. When she reached for it, he didn't let go. He said, "I knew the first time I saw you that there wouldn't be anything casual about sex with you."

God, she hated the way he could make her cheeks heat up and jumble her thoughts so she couldn't think of anything to say, witty or otherwise. He stood there, holding on to the phone and looking perfectly innocent, as though he were responding to a comment she'd made about the weather instead of sex. To avoid engaging in a tug-of-war over the phone, she had no choice but to wait until he let go.

"You know what amazes me?" he asked. "As long as you're talking about sex in the abstract, you don't bat an eye. But you blush like hell when it gets up close and personal. How long since you've been out on a date, Victoria?"

"I've had more important things to do with my time," she said, managing to find her voice again.

"Like sticking your nose in textbooks." He let go of the phone. "Answer the question. Have you been out on an honest-to-God, dinner-and-a-movie date since the divorce?"

Victoria studied the keypad of the telephone for a moment and decided that if they were going to play twenty questions, she was going to ask her fair share, too, when it was her turn. She tapped the phone against her thigh and said, "No, I haven't been out on a date in a while. I'll even tell you why, since my story is short and utterly predictable. It was a bad marriage, and I'm not eager to jump back in the saddle."

"So I'm paying for someone else's mistakes?"

"How do you know it wasn't all my fault?" she asked.

He shot her an irritated glare for sidestepping the original question. With one finger under her chin, he tilted her face up. "Was your marriage important to you?"

A prickly feeling ran up her spine, and Victoria had the strangest feeling that if she weren't careful, Joshua would see right into her soul. "Yes, it was."

"I believe you, because I saw you today, dealing with people, dealing with something that mattered to you. You're not the kind of woman who'd let her marriage slip through her fingers for lack of effort." Backing away, Joshua ordered, "Answer the question, Vicky. Am I paying for his mistakes or not?"

Victoria let out the breath she'd been holding. "Yeah, that about sums it up. Better safe than sorry is my new motto. What about you, Joshua? Why aren't you involved with someone? Or are you?"

For a heartbeat, Joshua thought about answering truthfully and telling her that he was involved with too many people, most of them dead. But he couldn't tell her without explaining, and he didn't want to explain yet.

"You're as close to an involvement as I've gotten in

a long time. I came up here to start over, to get a little peace and quiet."

"Then kissing me doesn't make a whole lot of sense!"

"Some things just happen, love. Whether we're ready for them or not. You surprised the hell out of me. The last complication I wanted was a woman. Then there you were, right smack in the middle of my bed. I figured the guy upstairs was trying to tell me something. What do you think it was?"

"I wouldn't begin to guess." Victoria decided it was time to end the questions, so she waved the phone in silent explanation that she needed to make the call. She punched in the number for her office. "Could I have some paper and a pencil?"

"On the end table behind you."

While Victoria waited for her machine to pick up and then replay the messages, she noticed the Indian arrowheads in shadowboxes on Joshua's walls. "Did you find all these yourself? There must be—"

"Over two hundred. I found most of them when I was a kid."

"They're beautiful," she mused as she stared at the largest of the boxes, which contained the head of a tomahawk flanked by arrowheads so pristine, they didn't look like they'd ever been used. "They're all so different."

"Different time periods. Different cultures. Different game to be hunted. Different skills."

Victoria wanted to ask more, but her messages started to play, and she had to forget about the shadowboxes. After a few minutes of writing she pulled the phone away from her ear and asked, "How do I hang this thing up?"

"Here. I'll do it."

When he reached for the receiver, he saw Victoria catch her breath. Joshua clicked the phone off and dropped into a large leather recliner that swallowed even him. "You can relax, Victoria. Now that I know the rules, I won't cross the line again until you invite me."

"Are you offering a truce?"

"I guess so. You haven't left me much choice." Joshua thought he saw some of the tension leave her as she put down the pencil and tore off the top sheet of paper on which she'd written her notes. As she folded the sheet, he suggested, "Sit down. Tell me what you think about the house. You're my first visitor."

"Do you want my honest opinion?"

"No. I want you to lie and say it's a great house."

"But it is." Victoria admired the long wall of windows on the far side of the room which looked out over the mountains. Unfortunately, the forested peaks were fading from view as night fell. "The scenery is remarkable, and the furniture is simply amazing. It's so . . . big."

"I had to have that sofa made to order."

Glancing at a piece of furniture that could have passed for a cruise ship, Victoria asked, "Why?"

"What good is a nap if you can't get comfortable because your feet are dangling over the edge?"

Victoria laughed. "I wouldn't know. I don't have that problem. My feet barely make it to the end of the sofa."

He remembered how he'd pulled her up to meet his kiss, how small she'd felt in his arms. "Yours may not, but mine definitely hang over."

"You shouldn't have to worry about that anymore." Victoria sat in the corner of the long sofa and crossed her legs.

He looked at her expectantly, prompting her with the lift of his eyebrows.

"Stop looking at me like that. I gave you my opinion. It's a great house. Really. I love rich earth tones. I think the Carol Grigg watercolors are incredible, especially the big one behind you of the Indian woman leading the horse. What's it called?"

"*She Walks with Horses.*" Joshua held his hand up in the Boy Scout oath. They both grinned.

"Appropriate. I've always admired her work. She has this gift for capturing the past and making you feel the moment with those moody shades of plum and blue—"

"I'm glad you like my taste in art," Joshua interrupted. "Now tell me what you really think about my house."

Victoria sighed. "Friend to friend? Real truth?"

"Real truth. I'm a big boy. I can take it."

"This house looks like it's waiting for someone to move in. Everything's too perfect, too new." She carefully folded her hands on her crossed knee and waited for his reaction.

"Tell me what you mean," he said, scooting to the edge of his seat.

"I grew up in houses like this. Mess it up a little, for God's sake. It's beautiful, but it's got no personality. I like a place you can walk into and feel vibrations from the memories. You should be able to sit in an easy chair and get a sense of what kind of person molded it. There's nothing of anybody here."

She missed the stunned look on Joshua's face at her comment because she got up and walked over to the shelves of cups and bowls, picking up a piece of the reproduction pottery. "Take these, for instance. They're lined up and lighted like museum pieces."

An odd smile turned up Joshua's mouth, and he stood to take the fat goblet from her. "That's because they are."

All the color drained from Victoria's face as she gently handed it to him. For a moment a memory flashed and then faded too quickly for her to grasp. Joshua returned the piece to the shelf.

"I'm so sorry." She stepped away from him. "I am so sorry. I thought a decorator found these to go with along with the arrowhead collection."

"No. They're mine."

"Is archaeology a hobby of yours?" Victoria asked, and tilted her head in interest. "Are you one of those amateur diggers?"

"Not really." Technically, that was true. It had been his occupation, not his avocation. He changed the subject before she could ask him where he'd gotten the artifacts. "Would you like to stay for dinner?"

"Oh, no." She checked her watch. "I should get ready for tomorrow. I've got my first appointments at the Bodewell clinic."

"There you go again. Doing what you should," he teased with a warm smile. "Maybe another time?"

"Yeah, that would be nice," Victoria said even though she knew spending time with Joshua wasn't a good idea. She said good night at the door and waved once when she pulled away in the truck.

Standing in the doorway, Joshua watched her go until her taillights had disappeared. What she'd said about his house was true. Except for books, the arrowheads, and the collection, everything was new. Brand new. He hadn't thought anyone but him would notice how sterile it was. But Victoria had. She'd seen it the moment she walked inside.

Maybe that was why she didn't trust him. Maybe she was worried that his house was a reflection of an empty soul. Regardless of the attraction between them, she wasn't ready to take another chance. She didn't trust him because she didn't know who he was; he could show her. She was warm, caring, intelligent, and nursing a bruised heart. She didn't want anything from him except friendship; well, that was a lot less than people usually expected of him. She was willing to be friends, but not lovers.

Joshua smiled. He could work with that.

Finally, the cabin felt like home. Victoria surveyed her efforts of the past two weeks. A chenille bedspread with a white background and climbing-rose floral design perked up the bedroom area. New throws which picked up the mauve and green of the bedspread covered the armchair and couch. The kitchen table had a plastic coaster under one leg to stabilize it, but Victoria didn't think it was noticeable.

Her pride and joy, however, was the new phone on the wrought iron bedside table. She'd waited what seemed like forever to have the lines run to the cabin, and she was itching to try it out.

"Who can I call?" she asked the empty cabin.

She didn't want to call home and have her mother ask her yet again if she was really happy. That left friends, but she didn't have any friends. At least not within this area code. She had patients and colleagues, but no real friends yet.

Except Joshua. Over the past couple of weeks, because of her busy appointment schedule, Victoria had tried to keep her thoughts about Joshua to a minimum. Except her thoughts weren't *friendly*. They went way beyond friendship. They went way beyond thoughts. Technically, they were daydreams. But he was still the only friend she had.

Giving in, she picked up the phone and dialed. After four rings he answered.

"Hello." His voice was rough and hoarse, as though she'd woken him from a nap. She could imagine him—shirtless, of course—grabbing the phone off the end table and pushing up to a sitting position on that long couch of his. Then he'd use his fingers to comb his hair out of his eyes.

"Hi," she said a little shakily, wondering what he'd do if he knew her thoughts. He'd made it abundantly clear that the only obstacle between them and an affair was her insistence that they were friends.

"Hi, yourself," he said, his voice snapping to attention. "Did we have plans?"

Victoria smiled and twirled the phone cord around her index finger. She could get used to the concern in his voice. It made her feel like she belonged. "No plans. The phone's all hooked up. I had to call somebody."

"Then I'm flattered it was my body you called."

She could feel the smile all the way through the phone. His voice did unbelievable things to her bones, and her reaction got worse every time she was around him. "Thanks for asking the crew to run my line on Saturday so I didn't have to cancel any appointments."

"I guess you owe me one."

"I guess I do." Victoria lay back on the bed. "I owe you several."

"What would you say if I told you that you could wipe the slate clean?"

"I'm all for that. What do I have to do? Rob the bank in Bodewell? Scrub your bathroom with my toothbrush?"

"Go to a dance with me." His voice reverberated through her as he said, "Tonight."

FIVE

Victoria sat up, one leg sliding off the bed and resting on the floor. "Tonight?"

"Yes, tonight. It's nothing fancy."

"But—"

"But nothing," Joshua interrupted. "It's an annual fund-raiser for the academic scholarship fund. What's the problem with a couple of friends showing up at the Harvest Dance together and having a good time? So . . . what do you say?"

"I thought you didn't like crowds," Victoria asked, scrambling for time. *A dance with Joshua. Bad idea, Victoria.*

"I don't, but you've turned down all of my friendly dinner invitations. I thought maybe a crowd would make you more comfortable."

"I don't know." She hesitated. "I'm not sure this is a good idea. Dancing? You and me?"

"It's the least you can do, Victoria. You have rattled my skeleton over every pothole in these mountains."

"You picked all the roads!"

"*And* you've forced me to sit on every porch between here and Knoxville. You owe me."

"But what—"

"Be ready at seven. Wear a dress."

"I haven't said—"

"Bye, Vicky."

Promptly at seven, Joshua knocked on the door, and Victoria scrambled to spray perfume and slip on her shoes at the same time. She hadn't been this nervous about a date in years. *It's not a date. It's two friends having some fun.*

"It's a date," she said under her breath. "Who do you think you're kidding? You're wearing your best dinner-and-dancing dress, for God's sake." She put on a smile and opened the door.

The smile fell immediately as she looked over Joshua's attire. He had on black cowboy boots that crinkled up a little bit at the toe, boot-cut faded jeans, and a crisp long-sleeved cotton shirt that was a patchwork of muted colors. He looked carelessly sexy, and she was dreadfully overdressed.

Forgoing the pleasantries, Victoria protested, "You said to wear a dress!"

"And it's a great dress," he commented as he glanced at the neckline. It was as far off the shoulder as a dress could get without actually being off the shoulder. The sweetheart neckline curved and dipped over her bust, and the fabric was a richly textured cream color that stopped mid-thigh. He repeated, "It's a great dress."

Seeing the laughter in his eyes, Victoria knew she'd been had. "That's not what I meant. We do not look like we are going to the same place. You deliberately misled me, didn't you?"

"So shoot me for wanting to see you all dressed up and shiny instead of wearing business clothes and your hair stuffed into a knot on top of your head! Would you have worn that if I'd told you that we were going to an old-fashioned meet-and-greet at the high school gym over in Mention?"

"Of course not!"

"Well, there you go." Joshua was clearly unrepentant.

"Shiny enough for you?" Victoria snapped, and swung her head in an imitation of shampoo ads.

Joshua answered with a slow, warm smile before he spoke. "You beat the hell out of moonlight on a clear night. And that's not easy to do. At least not by my standards. You ready?"

Joshua sounded so sincere, Victoria forgot about being irritated until she saw the motorcycle. "No. I'm not getting on that thing dressed like this. We'll take the truck."

"This is my shindig. I'm picking you up. Not the other way round. When you ask me out, you can drive the truck. Right now we take the cycle."

"I cannot believe you don't have a car."

"I do. It's in the shop. The transmission died a while back, and the mechanic had to order one because they don't stock something like that for foreign cars."

Putting her hands on her hips, Victoria asked reprovingly, "Haven't you heard of loaners?"

"They didn't have one, and I already had the cycle," he explained patiently. Part of him was testing her, trying to see how important her image was to her; trying to see if she cared about what people thought. The other part of him wanted her body resting on the back of his bike, curved around him. "Can we go now?"

Victoria paused and looked down at the straight skirt of her dress, wondering how awkward it would be to sit on the back of the bike. She laughed at herself for even considering it. "Are you blind? I can't get on that thing. Not in this dress."

"Sure you can. I'll bring the bike right alongside the steps, and you can slide on behind me. What could be easier?"

"Getting my truck keys." Victoria crossed her arms, prepared to hold her ground.

"I've got two helmets. Come on, Vicky. You owe me."

"No, I don't. Going to the dance evens the score. You didn't say anything about my having to ride on this machine when we struck the bargain. If you want me to get on that contraption, you're going to have to do me a favor."

"I'd love to do you . . . a favor."

Victoria let out a gasp at his innuendo.

"Something wrong?" Joshua asked innocently.

Smart enough to avoid trouble, Victoria didn't explain her reaction. Ever since Joshua asked her to the dance, thinking of him as just a friend had become hopeless unless the emotions allowed between friends were revised to include lust. She grabbed her purse from the shelf by the door and locked up the cabin.

"Look, I'll sacrifice my dignity and ride on your motorcycle if you help me track down a granny-midwife that might still be alive. One of my patients couldn't remember the name, but said there was a mountain midwife actually practicing up until about fifteen years ago. I've been meaning to ask Dr. Grenwald, but he and Helen took that vacation to Minnesota to see their newest great-grandbaby."

Apprehension tightened Joshua's shoulders as he watched her slip the key in her purse. *A granny was practicing until fifteen years ago when I left the mountains, and she didn't have a way to visit her patients anymore.* The last thing he wanted to do was help Victoria find his ninety-two-year-old grandmother, who kept *Touching History* prominently displayed on her coffee table. It was a miracle that he'd been able to keep his alter ego from Victoria this long.

He was going to the dance in Mention only because he didn't have much contact with anyone there. What little family he had left in the mountains lived around the Logan's Hollow point of the triangle. He doubted he would be recognized at a crowded gathering of people who weren't expecting *the* Joshua Logan to drop in on their festivities.

He'd be safe tonight, but once Victoria met his grandmother, the charade would be over. He'd spent a great deal of time in the past few years feeling like a bug under glass. He didn't want to go back to that. Not yet anyway. He hated the thought that once Victoria put two and two together, she would begin to look at him in that dissecting way that medical people had, trying to figure out if he was a fake or simply crazy. He didn't want his grandmother subjected to that kind of scrutiny either.

As he casually descended the steps and threw a leg over the gleaming black motorcycle, he made a decision. If Victoria was going to find his grandmother, she'd have to do it on her own, without help from him. He maneuvered the bike into position beside the bottom step and held out his hand to steady Victoria as he asked, "Why do you want to waste time talking to someone who hasn't delivered a baby in fifteen years?"

Victoria widened her eyes at his negative attitude. "Waste of time? How can you say that? You grew up here. The Appalachians are the oldest mountains on this continent. Some of the oldest healing in America is centered right here. You betcha I want to track this woman down if she's alive." While she talked, Victoria put her hand in his, held the edge of her dress, and eased onto the motorcycle behind him. "Think of what she can teach me about folk medicine. She'd actually have used herbal medicine instead of repeating what someone told her. Think of how many babies the woman delivered, how many problems she's faced, how much she knows that can't be learned from books."

Joshua handed her a helmet, silently cursing the enthusiasm he heard in her voice. She wasn't going to be easily discouraged, but he tried anyway. "Fifteen years is a long time, and she was already an old woman when she retired."

"You know her?" Victoria exclaimed, stopping in the middle of putting on the headgear.

Joshua winced, glad she couldn't see his face. "No. I figure she had to be old if she retired."

"Oh," she said, her enthusiasm dampened but not gone. "Well . . . I still want to try."

Turning the key, Joshua let the noise of the engine drown out his need to give her an answer. "Hold on."

Victoria forgot the conversation as soon as the bike lurched forward and up the hill. Instantly, her arms went around Joshua's chest of their own accord. Safety was obviously more important to her subconscious than her pride, which wanted her to keep a safe distance from the heat of his body.

When her arms circled him so naturally, Joshua smiled. He was going to enjoy this ride even more than he usually did. Telling the mechanic not to deliver his car yet had been a calculated risk, but worth it.

Neither of them tried to talk. Joshua knew shouting against the roar of wind and engine was futile; Victoria wanted Joshua's full attention to be focused on the road. The first few minutes she kept her eyes closed, not wanting to see the sheer drops on her right. Gradually she opened them and began to enjoy the incredible feeling of freedom.

The air teased her as it rushed over Joshua's shoulders, catching the stray ends of hair she hadn't managed to stuff into the helmet. When she burrowed her face against his back, she breathed in the scent that she associated with Joshua—woodsy, clean, strong. Beneath her fingers she could feel the muscles of his abdomen bunch and twist as he used his body to control the motorcycle through the turns.

Gradually, Victoria realized that riding behind Joshua was the sensual equivalent to being given a license to steal. So what if she accidentally pressed her breasts to his back and her hands slipped to his waist and hips? It wasn't her fault. Joshua had wanted to take the bike. So what if the bumps and turns in the road jostled them until she thought she couldn't take another minute of rubbing against him? Too soon and yet not soon enough, the mountain road began to twist and curve in the downward descent toward Mention.

Joshua slowed the bike as he approached the smallest of the three Triangle anchor towns. Mention boasted a population of only about two thousand people, but was fortunate to have persuaded the school board to build a brand-new county high school in their community. A grocery store, two gas/convenience stores, a tiny motel, a Dairy Ice Hut, and a business selling concrete yard statues were about the only buildings on the main drag. He bypassed them all and pulled into the high school.

Carefully he stopped the bike close to the curb that edged the school driveway and killed the engine. As soon as he did, Victoria dropped her hands and pulled away from him. Shaking his head, he wondered what he was going to have to do to get Victoria to give in to the physical side of her nature. He knew it was there. He'd seen flashes of it before she could disguise it.

"We're here," he announced.

"I can see that." Victoria placed her hands on his shoulders. "You sit right where you are while I get off."

"I was going to help you," he teased.

"Oh, please. I can just picture that. Thank you, but no thank you. I'd prefer to crawl off this bike without an audience."

His laughter rang out into the growing darkness as he took off his helmet. "Baby, you've got an audience. Take a look around."

Surreptitiously, Victoria glanced toward the two double doors opening into the gym. Seven or eight gentlemen were gathered on the sidewalk, taking a smoke break. Every one of them was looking in her direction. "I can't believe this. I should never have gotten on this bike."

"There you go again. Thinking about what you should and shouldn't do."

"I should have tried to get a loan from some city in Iowa," Victoria told him sharply. "I'm sure they wouldn't have stuck me with a guide who has a rebel-without-a-cause motorcycle fixation."

Gingerly, she rested the toe of her shoe on the curb and slowly shifted her weight to it. Standing up, she tugged her dress as far down as she could and still swing her leg over the back of the motorcycle as if she were dismounting a horse. "Okay, I'm off."

Joshua turned his head toward her and then wished he hadn't. The rustle of material and the shimmy of her body as she readjusted the fit of the dress was torture. What bothered him the most was that she didn't have a clue what she was doing to him. To Victoria it was a gesture to recover her modesty; to Joshua the movement was downright erotic. Adding insult to injury, she unbuckled the helmet and shook out her thick, glossy hair, drawing his eyes to her pale shoulders as the windblown curls settled around her neck and covered her collarbones.

Finally, she held out the helmet and gave him a ingenuous smile. "I hate to admit it, but that was kind of fun."

"Wait until we do it in the dark," Joshua told her with a devilish look as he secured the helmets and got off the bike.

"Wh-what?"

Joshua put his arm around her waist and walked her toward the gym. "Don't worry. I have excellent night vision. I hardly ever drive off the edge."

"Stop scaring me," she complained, and slapped him lightly on the chest.

"I'll add that to the list."

"What list?"

"Things a person should and should not do according to Victoria Bennett."

"I'm not that bad," she defended herself as they walked up the fanlike steps.

Joshua didn't say anything.

"Am I?" she asked uncertainly.

"Let's just say that the list keeps getting longer."

While Victoria mulled over his comment, he paid the entry fee to the teenage girl who sat behind the ticket table in the gym lobby. The teenager lowered her blond head as she rummaged in the old metal box to make change for his twenty.

"Hope you don't mind ones," she said with a bright smile as she counted out ten of them. "It's all I have."

Joshua noticed her name badge, which read LISA STONE—HONORABLE MENTION SCHOLAR. "How much are you trying to raise this year?" he asked as he opened his wallet to put the cash away.

"Three thousand. The top three seniors get to split the interest on the fund and half of what we raise this year." She hesitated softly, "I finished fifth my junior year."

"Do you think you'll raise that much this year?" Victoria asked.

"Hope so. It's a lot of money, all right, but if we raise more than that, we might be able to include more students than just the top three." She smiled. "That would make me feel better about my chances."

Joshua fished out a business card and held it out.

"You have the head of the committee give me a call. Maybe I can help you reach your goal this year."

The girl took the card, her eyes widening. A chill went through Joshua, and he knew he'd made a mistake. Quietly, he waited for the inevitable.

"But you live in Bodewell," Lisa read from the card. "They have a high school too. Are you sure you want to give us your money?"

Breathing a sigh of relief, Joshua grinned. "Absolutely. You have someone give me a call first thing Monday. In fact, have your parents give me a call. Okay?"

"Yes, sir!" Joshua grabbed Victoria's hand and led her toward the sound of soft, slow music. The girl called after them, "They don't want high heels on the gym floor, but anything else is okay, Mr. Logan."

The lights were dim, and the gym was decorated with streamers. A concession stand was set up between the two locker room doors on the opposite wall. About a hundred adult couples were scattered throughout the room, some sitting in groups on the bleachers, others dancing to music that must have been taped, since Victoria couldn't see a band or a disc jockey.

"Hey, that was pretty nice of you," she said softly as she slipped off her high heels and gave them to the tall, lanky kid manning the shoe-check booth. "Giving that girl your card and promising to help."

"She'll lose the card before she gets home. Trust me."

"Right," Victoria said sarcastically.

"Well, what was I supposed to do? Go home and worry that she'd get left out, when a few bucks could make the difference?"

"Most people would."

"I'm not most people," he told her, using her favorite comeback.

"I've noticed, and I'm not complaining," Victoria told him happily as she took in the homespun atmosphere and heard the laughter coming from all over the room. "You know, I'm used to dressy affairs in posh hotels with unappetizing appetizers. Even when I was a teenager the dances were kind of stuffy and formal. This is better. Much better. I'll bet your prom was a little like this."

"Wouldn't know. I didn't go."

She turned to gape at him. Joshua didn't strike her as the kind of man who had blossomed late in life. He had the kind of good looks that began with boyish charm and only got better. "Do not expect me to believe that you couldn't get a date."

"I probably could have gotten a date," he admitted.

"Then why didn't you go?"

"I didn't go to dances."

"Why not?"

"I don't like crowds," Joshua said. He avoided them whenever he could. Tonight's foray into the throng was forced on him by Victoria's refusal to take their relationship to the next logical step.

"But you're here tonight. So how can you say you

don't like crowds?" she asked as he led her onto the floor.

"Because it's true. I'm not crazy about crowds."

"Why not?" she asked, intrigued.

Joshua didn't answer right away. He was more concerned with the effortless way she flowed into his arms and followed his lead. His fingers curled around her hand and drew it to his chest. His thigh rode between hers as he caught the rhythm of the music. All of his senses were engaged in the reality of holding Victoria.

For a moment he didn't even notice that he wasn't catching the emotional echoes of the people around him. When the silence hit him, he realized that he'd centered all his awareness on Victoria, so much so that he had been able to tune out the rest of the world for once. He was trying to read her as he held her close, trying to finally get some sense of who she was inside. Nothing else had been important.

Still not answering her question about his dislike of crowds, Joshua rested his cheek against the top of her head and filled his lungs with the light, springtime scent she wore tonight. Unhappily, he accepted the fact that no matter how hard he tried, he couldn't feel Victoria the way he could other people. It was as though she'd erected a privacy fence around her deepest emotions so that none of them spilled onto him.

Until a few weeks ago, if he'd been asked to describe the kind of woman he thought he could make a life with, the number-one requirement would have been an emotional privacy fence. Victoria should have been exactly the kind of woman he wanted. Now he wasn't sure. Not being able to grasp her feelings, yet holding her physically, disturbed him.

"Okay, so you're tight-lipped about your phobias," she said, breaking his train of thought.

Joshua chuckled. "Isn't everyone?"

"I suppose."

He pulled back to look down at her. "I'll tell you mine if you tell me yours."

She grinned and clutched him tight as he abruptly dipped her. When she caught her breath, she said, "My phobia is getting stuck with a dance partner who dips."

"How unfortunate," Joshua commiserated, but his expression was full of mischief as he righted her and danced a few more steps. "I don't like crowds because it's too damn hard to dip when you're dancing."

"That's a lie."

"Of course it is. You don't think I'm going to tell you all my deep, dark secrets on our first date, do you?"

"I was hoping," Victoria said.

He dipped her again. "I never tell my secrets."

The moment of gentle teasing subsided as Victoria realized, that despite his flippant attitude, he did have secrets. She could see it in his eyes. She'd seen it that first day in the cabin, that subtle hint of mystery hiding behind a crooked grin.

"Want something to drink?" Joshua asked to forestall the questions he saw creeping into her expression. He lifted her up without breaking eye contact. "I think the strongest thing they'll have at the concession stand is root beer."

Shaken by her conclusions, Victoria quietly answered, "Root beer's fine with me."

Joshua wove them through the other dancers and gestured to an empty spot of bleacher. "You rest your bones, and I'll go get the drinks."

"Rest my bones!" she exclaimed. "You make me sound like an insipid debutante who needs a Long Island tea and a fan after a trip to the mailbox!"

"You did say you were from Connecticut," he tossed over his shoulder.

"Were," Victoria called after him as he disappeared in the crowd. "*Were* is the operative word in that sentence!" She was still brooding about his remark when he returned with drinks in hand. For some reason, he had touched a nerve she hadn't even known was raw. Before she could stop herself, she told him point blank, "I am not a snob or a . . . a dilettante playing at being a midwife. This is what I do. Who I am now."

"Hey, take it easy." Surprised at the passion in her voice, Joshua frowned as he handed her the soft drink. "You say that like you have trouble convincing people."

"Maybe I do," she admitted, and self-consciously stirred her root beer with the straw. "Sorry. I guess that was simply a knee-jerk reaction on my part. You didn't deserve a lecture. I know you were teasing, but I am so tired of everyone expecting me to be a certain way because of my background."

"What do they expect you to be?"

"More like them and less like me, I guess. Richard expected me to continue to vegetate on the country-club circuit because my mother and his mother always had. My parents remind me at every opportunity that I'm not cut out for this. Although they'd probably change their minds if money or recognition were involved. Daddy loves the rich, and Mother loves the famous. They were hoping I'd be both. Richard had political aspirations."

Very casually, Joshua asked, "How do you feel about that? Money and fame?"

"It's probably a nice gig if you can get it." Then she shrugged. "But neither of them is usually associated with my chosen profession."

Her answer didn't satisfy Joshua. He'd known too many women who were interested only in a page for their scrapbook. For some reason, he wanted a definite answer from her. He wanted some idea of how she'd react to who he was when she found out. He wanted Victoria not to care. He wanted to believe she would be surprised but not particularly impressed. "Then you can live without fame and fortune?"

She looked at him oddly. "I'll have to. I'm not giving up catching babies for money and marriage. And unless you can come up with a way to turn me into a celebrity midwife, it looks like I'll have to be happy just the way I am."

While he was glad to know she wasn't chasing notoriety, Joshua found himself questioning an unexpected comment. "You've ruled out marriage? One strike and you're out? Is that it?"

"No." Victoria sipped her drink. "I've just found that most men feel midwives are too intense. We are too prone to actually expect communication and support." She grinned at the floor and wiggled her pink-tipped toes. "Most men run like rabbits from midwives. You guys don't like sharing. You get cranky when we have to crawl out of bed in the middle of the night."

"If you want to talk about sharing, let's talk about you and that truck of yours!"

"It's my truck," she told him. The fight was an old and comfortable one by now.

Joshua didn't bother to argue. He took the cup out of her hand and put both drinks on the bleachers. "They're playing our song."

"Friends don't have songs."

"We're not friends," he told her seriously as he stood up. "At least friends is not all we are if you're honest with yourself."

His tone of voice sent a shiver up Victoria's spine. He was challenging her. They both knew what he said was true, but he wanted to hear her admit it. Somehow it was important to him. Victoria stumbled over saying the words. Once she confessed her feelings for him, they'd eventually end up in bed. Maybe not tonight. Maybe not next week. But eventually.

The only protection she had was the façade of friendship between them. Brush that aside and she would be emotionally naked.

"I'm not sure I want to be more than friends," she said, picking her words carefully. "I'm not sure I'm ready."

"Who the hell ever is?" he asked gently, and pulled her up. "Dance with me and let what we are to each other take care of itself."

"That's what I'm afraid of," she whispered.

"No," Joshua corrected her, and led her onto the floor. He cupped her face with his hands and dropped a kiss on her parted lips. "You're afraid of letting anyone inside. Just like the rest of us."

He might not be able to read her mind, but he listened. He had a fair idea of Victoria's problems, and they included being afraid of disappointment. That was a fear they shared. Both of them had been burned.

The kiss made him hungry for more, but the dance floor wasn't the place to indulge himself. He let the motion of the dance do what he couldn't right now. He came as close as he dared to making love to a woman in a public place without raising eyebrows.

He made sure that her breasts were lightly touching his chest. He liked the anticipation as they brushed against him unexpectedly, rubbing him. Victoria liked it too. Her face was flushed, and she sucked in a tiny breath each time contact was made.

Halfway through the song, Victoria knew they weren't doing much more than wearing a hole in the floor and swaying, but she didn't care. For once in her life she was attracted to a man who made her feel as though they had all the time in the world to explore each other. His hand trailed down her back and pressed her hips against his. She closed her eyes as her belly met the full extent of his arousal.

When Victoria wiggled against him, Joshua gritted his teeth. Once he'd worked his way to the edge of the dance floor, he said quietly, "We're leaving. Now."

Letting her eyes drift open, Victoria saw the passion in his. She liked that feeling of power, as though she had as much control over his reactions as he had over hers. Leaving was just fine by her. He wasn't going to kiss her the way she wanted to be kissed as long as they were in public. "My shoes."

"I'll get them. It may take a while to find them."

"I'll wait right here."

Inane conversation, but Victoria knew it said, in code, everything they wanted to say—"I don't want you to change your mind." "I won't."

Her mind was already skipping ahead to the motorcycle ride and the intimacy it created, when a woman's voice broke her train of thought.

"Ms. Bennett?"

Forcing her irritation to go away, Victoria told herself that no one else could possibly know they were interrupting a fantasy. She turned and was pleasantly surprised. "Naomi! How many times do I have to tell you to call me Victoria?"

The woman shrugged. "I'll try. It's hard though."

"Why's that?"

"Well, the other granny was older. I ain't much used to someone close to my age."

Victoria's eyebrows shot up, and she felt the

adrenaline surge through her body. "The other midwife?"

"Yeah, the one Ma used."

Victoria closed her eyes for a second and crossed her fingers. "You don't happen to remember her name, do you? I'd like to find her and talk to her."

The pregnant woman's brow furrowed. "I was only eight when she came the last time." She worried her lip with her teeth. Suddenly Naomi's face cleared, and she nodded. "It was Granny Logan, I think. Don't recollect the first name, but the last name was Logan."

SIX

"Logan?" All the excitement rushed out of Victoria. If the midwife's last name had been Logan, wouldn't Joshua have known her? He was a Logan who grew up in the mountains. He seemed to know a great deal about the different families in the mountains, almost as if someone had taught him local history and folklore. He ought to have known a midwife named Logan, but Victoria couldn't think of any reason Joshua would lie.

Knowing that the memories of eight-year-olds weren't always reliable, Victoria asked, "Are you absolutely sure?"

"I think . . . so." Naomi frowned as if afraid to guarantee her recollection now that she thought about it seriously. "I'm almost positive anyway. But I could ask Ma if you want. She'd remember for sure. She might even remember where the woman lived."

Excited again, Victoria touched the other woman's elbow. "Would you mind?"

Naomi shook her head. "No. I'll call Ma tomorrow when we get back from Sunday meetin'. I'd be proud to help. I appreciate what you done for me."

"I haven't done anything yet," Victoria disagreed.

"You're helpin' us get that insurance."

"All I did was mention that your husband qualified for the COBRA insurance continuation when his company laid him off. His company should have told him about it to start with."

"Don't much matter how it happened, Victoria. All I know is that I can sleep at night 'cause I'm not fretted about my baby no more. Or how I'm going to get a doctor without having the money to pay for the birthin' till the insurance gets straightened out."

"You pay what you can. Everything else will work itself out." Victoria smiled, thinking about the dance with Joshua a few minutes earlier. "It usually does whether you want it to or not."

Naomi smiled back and said her good-byes with a promise to call as soon as she had more information about the granny-midwife. When Naomi turned away, Joshua appeared at her side, looking at the pregnant woman with a glimmer of recognition in his eyes.

"Wasn't she your first house call?"

"Yeah. That was Naomi. She's going to research that midwife I'm trying to find. Her mother knows—" Victoria broke off as he gave her a mock bow and held out her shoes.

"My prince," Victoria teased, and took the pumps as he steered her toward the lobby.

"Let's hope you still feel that way when you really get to know me." *Or when you find out that your midwife is my grandmother, and that I won't allow anyone to put her under a microscope the way I was.*

She patted his arm and followed him off the dance floor. "I learned a long time ago that real princes exist only in fairy tales." Standing in the foyer, Victoria braced a hand against his shoulder and lifted each foot to slip on her shoes. "The last time I looked, my life was not a fairy tale, so I promise not to be disappointed when you turn back into a frog."

"And I promise not to turn into a frog too quickly." Joshua pulled her out into the night, which had cooled enough for Victoria to rub her arms. As if he'd been doing it for years, Joshua slipped his arm around her and settled her next to his body. "I've got a light jacket in the seat of the bike. But until we get there, I guess you'll have to rely on me."

"What a concept," she quipped. "Having someone to rely on. Do you suppose it's possible?"

"You'll never know unless you try," he warned her.

Victoria's hand slid around his waist of its own volition, and they walked entwined to the motorcycle. Verbal conversation ceased, but their bodies began to talk. Their hips bumped and rubbed lightly against each other as they made their way down the steps.

Victoria couldn't recall feeling so safe and warm. His presence enveloped her, made her aware of the height and breadth of the man. Of the heat of his body. Of the possibility that the night would end in intimacy.

She couldn't pinpoint the moment when she had finally given up thinking of Joshua as just a friend. The hours they'd spent together would have taken up two months of dating in the real world, but she still wasn't sure she knew him well enough. Oh, she knew *him*—that he hated salads and liked his hamburgers with everything; that he preferred prewashed faded jeans; that all the clothes she'd seen him in were natural fabrics; that he was a sucker for shirts in rich brown or gold or burgundy; that he loved the mountains; and a million other details—but she didn't know about *his past*. All she knew was that he didn't have much family left in the area, that he didn't appear to need money, and that he was retired from some vague enterprise that required travel around the world.

Dr. Grenwald had called him a man she could trust with a secret. At the time it seemed an odd comment, since she didn't have any secrets. Now she understood what he meant. Joshua Logan was an honorable man. He kept his word. He had earned respect.

All these details were more important than a biography, but she couldn't shake years of hearing her mother say, "You can never know too much about a man, Victoria. People make bad choices because they don't have the right information." Hadn't she made a mistake with Richard because she hadn't asked what he wanted out of marriage?

Tonight she should have asked Joshua more questions, made him talk more about himself, what he wanted, and his past. But he always seemed to steer the conversation in the opposite direction. Common sense told her that she should call a halt to the rush of excitement that ripped through her as his fingers stroked her bare arm while they walked. But knowing and doing didn't always go together.

For once it was nice to do what she wanted and not what she *should*. She wanted to believe in possibilities and not worry about getting too close and the risk of trusting another man with her emotions. She wanted to get on that motorcycle of his and let the wind blow all the bad memories out of her head and—Victoria almost stumbled as she realized why Joshua had the bike. You couldn't think on a bike. Not when it was going that fast. Not about anything but the road.

She wondered what bad memories he was chasing away. Unconsciously, she hugged him a little tighter. She understood all about getting away from the past.

Joshua felt the gentle squeeze from Victoria. He looked down at the top of her head which lay against his chest as they walked. He felt a momentary stab of guilt at the trust she was placing in him, considering the secrets he was keeping and how little he'd told her of himself. Time was running out. He'd have to tell her soon. The new book was coming out next month.

Carefully, Joshua disengaged himself and pulled a windbreaker from the compartment beneath the seat of the motorcycle. Shaking it out, he offered it to her and waited as she slid into it and reached to straighten the collar. He noticed the almost imperceptible quiver of her hands as he brushed them aside to do it for her.

In that split second, as their hands touched, the emotions of fear and lust stabbed through him. The emotions weren't his. They were Victoria's. For the first time he'd made a connection, even though it was transitory. He pushed, but the wall around her was firmly in place again.

"It unnerves you when I touch you, doesn't it? I mean, more than you're used to," he murmured. The knowledge rekindled his desire to the intensity he'd felt on the dance floor. "More than you want to admit. Even to yourself."

Victoria lifted her chin and cleared her throat. "Joshua, I'm not a starry-eyed virgin."

Her skin was soft beneath his fingers, and he could tell that she was holding her breath. "Then don't act like one. Love, I want the woman I see glimpses of. The one who shakes because she's afraid of shocking me. You're holding back. All the time. I'm tired of playing hide-and-seek, Victoria. Try to shock me." His gaze roamed hungrily. "You might learn something about yourself."

With as much control as she could muster, Victoria tried to ignore the magic of his feathery touches and said, "I don't need a lesson in lovemaking. I know what an orgasm is." Sarcastically she added, "I've even had one."

He traced the line of her collarbone, the length of her neck, and rubbed his thumb across her bottom lip.

"With someone else in the room?" Joshua asked softly.

Stunned, Victoria couldn't frame a reply.

"I want to be in the room, Victoria. You understand? I want you, and I don't care what you know or what you don't know as long as you're honest about what you want." Joshua kissed her quickly, softly. "I'll go first. I'll be honest about what I want. I want more than friendship." He ran his hands down over her breasts, and she arched into his palms.

Not responding to her wordless plea, Joshua moved his hands to her waist. He wanted her to let go of her emotions and admit her sensual nature, but this wasn't the place. He wanted privacy. Slowly he withdrew his hands and asked, "Ready?"

Victoria nodded, unwilling to trust her voice, and waited for Joshua to retrieve the helmets and get on first. Then she tugged her skirt up until she could slip on behind him. The moment her bottom touched the seat, Joshua started the engine. She almost gasped at the effect the vibration had on her. It echoed sensually through her, making her feel empty and aching, making her remember the blunt way he asked for what he wanted and the funny sensation she got deep in her belly when he told her. Heat flooded not only her cheeks but the juncture of her thighs.

Closing her eyes, Victoria swallowed and wondered how she was going to manage the long ride home. More than that, she wondered if Joshua was as affected as she was by the fleeting feel of his big hands against her breasts and by the power rumbling beneath them. She wondered if he was translating those sensations to mental images that only made the need worse.

As he made adjustments before driving away, he pushed himself firmly between her thighs and ordered, "Get a grip."

With no more warning than that, he roared off. If the ride during dusk had been unsettling, the ride in the dark was devastating. Nothing existed in the blackness except the feel of his body beneath her hands. Her mother would have called the way her skirt was hiked up indecent, but Victoria was past caring. All she knew was that the man in front of her wanted her to let go. That he told her with a thousand tiny clues to forget the world. He was sharing something with her, sharing his need to forget.

Richard had never shared anything with her, least of all sensual pleasure. He wanted a body in bed; he'd never wanted her. Not really. She knew that now. Richard made her beg for scraps, while Joshua offered whatever she wanted. Except his past.

The night air whipped around them, cool and crisp, carrying the smell of fall. Victoria realized that even nature recognized a time to move on, a time to change, a time to strip yourself bare so you could begin again. Maybe it was time she let down the walls some.

By the time they were halfway home, Victoria's hands were moving across Joshua's flat belly, soaking up the warmth and the feel of his muscles. She ran her palms up the washboard of his abdomen and grazed his nipples with her fingers. His body grew taut, but he didn't flinch away, didn't tell her to stop. And his nipples hardened beneath her assault.

Victoria wanted to touch him, wanted to learn the landscape of his body as well as she knew her own. She reveled in his response to her. Something about riding hell-bent-for-leather in the black of night created a whole new set of rules for her, gave her permission to do things she might not have done otherwise.

Just as the ride to the dance ended too soon, so did the ride home. Joshua slowed the bike and turned into Victoria's driveway, coasting up beside the porch. When he switched off the engine, the silence was deafening.

Suddenly, the anonymity of the night ride slipped away. Victoria's heart raced, knowing she couldn't hide any longer. She was going to have to look him in the face and acknowledge that she wanted him as much as he wanted her. Joshua pushed the helmet off his head and ran his fingers through his hair.

"Want to come in?" she asked tentatively, cursing the waver in her voice.

Without turning around he asked, "Do you want me to come in?"

"I don't want you to go home," she said honestly, and got off the bike as gracefully as she could, considering her nerves. She took her helmet off and handed it to him.

"Then I guess I'll come in." Joshua shifted his gaze to her. His blue eyes glinted briefly, but she couldn't tell if it was the moonlight or anticipation that caused the change. Joshua followed her to the door, stopping her with a light touch on her shoulder as she unlocked and opened it. "You have something that belongs to me."

"Oh," she said as she remembered the jacket.

When she turned and looked up, he cupped her head in his hands and gave her the kiss he'd wanted to give her on the dance floor. His lips didn't ease over hers this time. His mouth covered hers swiftly and completely, his tongue sweeping inside to take possession without waiting for invitation. One hand slipped around to the back of her neck and the other slid down the column of her throat.

She arched into him, and Joshua swept the windbreaker off her shoulders and down her arms, pinning her to the doorframe. Everything about her signaled her consent, encouragement even, to being picked up and carried to the bed. He could still remember what she looked like lying on it, stretching her sexy body like a contented cat. He wanted to sink inside her and satisfy himself, making love hard and furious and fast, but he also knew Victoria wasn't ready for that. Not yet.

Despite her sensual nature, she was still far from experienced. If he took her too quickly or too roughly, she wouldn't come with him, and he wanted her with him every step of the way. He wanted to be inside her when she climaxed. Maybe then he'd know what Victoria really felt like. Maybe then he could touch her soul and discover what it was that drew him to her like a hawk to its one true mate.

Victoria struggled to get her hands out of the jacket and around his neck to press herself closer, but Joshua pushed her away. "Wait. This is too fast. Too quick, love. Got any objections if I slow this down?"

Frustration hummed in every pore of Victoria's being. Disappointment was evident in her tone as she breathlessly responded, "You want to slow down?"

"Yeah, as in—I won't last two seconds if I let you do anything else to me just yet. You near did me in on the bike ride, Vicky. I'm having a hard time holding on to my good intentions here."

Joshua's gruff confession erased her frustration instantly. She handed him the jacket and backed into the dark cabin, dropping her purse and key inside the front door. "I always hated good intentions. You know what they say about them."

He tossed the jacket in the direction of the bike. "Actually mine are more like dishonorable intentions."

"I was hoping," Victoria whispered, but she made one last halfhearted effort to stop the inevitable. "You know that making love is probably the best way to wreck a friendship. We might regret this in the morning. At least I might. We've built a friendship that means something to me."

"We've been marking time until you were ready, love. And you know it." As she backed up, he followed, kicking the door shut with a well-placed boot heel.

Victoria got rid of her shoes. "How can you know me so well? How could you be so sure I was ready, when I didn't even admit it to myself until tonight?" she whispered, and stopped retreating when the backs of her thighs touched the bed.

"Know you? In some ways I don't feel like I know you at all," Joshua told her as he closed the distance. "And it's driving me crazy. You see, I usually know things about people. But not about you. Who are you really, Vicky?" His fingers trailed along her neck, seeking and finding the erratic pulse at the base of her throat. "Why did you show up on my mountain just when I'd decided I could live without complications in my life?"

He kissed her again. When his arms went around her, he found the zipper of her dress and slowly drew it down to the sweet curve of her back. His fingers toyed with the valley formed by the arch of her back as she leaned into him. A sigh escaped her as he began to press kisses along the side of her neck, finding her pulse with his mouth this time.

Her dress began to slide off her shoulders, and Joshua helped it on its way until the gentle flare of her hips stopped the descent. By then her lace-covered breasts were bared to his gaze, and took all his attention. He wondered if she'd worn this particular bra on purpose. It was strapless and revealed more than it covered or supported. Creamy flesh flowed over the pristine white edges, begging him to touch and to release her.

Joshua gave up and swept Victoria back on the bed. There was a limit to what any man could take. He waited only long enough to dispose of his boots and shirt before joining her. Lace scraped against his chest as he pulled her to him and hooked his fingers in a cup and dragged it down to expose her breast. The catch in Victoria's breathing was audible as his mouth covered the passion-darkened tip.

Fireworks exploded in Victoria as Joshua sucked at her, pulling and laving her nipple with an expertise that began an insistent throbbing between her legs. His hands were as big as she had fantasized; he could cup her breast completely, plumping it as he created a rock-hard peak.

Her hips were beginning to move when he gave the nipple one last caress before peeling back the cup hiding the other breast from his view. Cold air teased the first bud, and she could feel the second growing hard as he gazed at her.

"Joshua . . ." His name was all she could get out, but she wanted him to touch her again, to finish what he had started without all this waiting and teasing.

"Easy, love. The party's not going anywhere." He ran an index finger around the inside of her panty hose and slip. "These, however, have to go."

Joshua stripped them off and also unhooked her bra, tossing it on the floor with the other unnecessary items. Victoria was naked except for high-cut white panties which he found incredibly sexy. Lace, like that on the bra, fluttered invitingly along the diagonal line from the edge of her hip to the triangle between her legs.

He still had his jeans on, but he unbuttoned the waistband, and under the wide-eyed gaze of Victoria he unzipped. He could tell she enjoyed it. She liked the bits and pieces of sex. She liked the details. He made himself another promise to take this as slow as he could.

The bed squeaked a protest as he reached for her hands and pulled her up until she was on her knees, facing him. He eased his arousal out of his pants and then brought her close. They were thigh to thigh, belly to belly, and heat to heat. For the first time, her bare breasts made contact with his bare chest.

Wanting to see how the whisper of flesh against flesh affected her, he said, "Open your eyes, Vicky."

Surprisingly, she didn't ease them open uncertainly. She opened them instantly at his request, looking down first at the sight of their bodies touching, then up to his mouth, and finally into his eyes. The intensity in her expression blew him away. How could she experience emotions this powerful without echoes spilling over into his mind? For a moment he wondered what it would take before she let him inside. Not just physically, but emotionally. And if he could deal with the intimacy when she did.

When her head tilted back so she could see him more clearly, her hair tumbled down her back, teasing his arms as he held her close. She was gorgeous. He flattened his palms against her back and slid his hands down to the curve of her hip. Victoria caught her breath but didn't look away as he slipped his hands inside the high-cut legs of her panties and cupped her bottom. Gently he kneaded her tender flesh and lifted her against him.

The shrill shriek of the phone bell, turned up on high, jarred the mood and forced a curse from Joshua as Victoria almost jumped out of his arms. He leaned his forehead against hers. "Don't answer it."

"I . . . I have to," she told him shakily, trying to regulate her breathing and erase the husky aftermath of passion from her voice. "Might be the answering service."

Joshua moved aside and adjusted his clothing while she answered the phone. Modesty motivated her to grab a crocheted afghan that hung over the end of the bed.

"Hello," she said as she tucked the holey concoction of yarn around her like a shawl. "Who? Oh. Sorry, I wasn't expecting the hospital to call." Victoria listened for a while and then flipped on the Tiffany-style lamp beside her bed to look at her watch. "Yeah, that sounds about right. She's a patient of Dr. Grenwald's. He left her file with me, since she was the only possible delivery while he was out of town."

As soon as she flipped on the light, Joshua's heart sank. He'd lost her for the night. A wry grin crossed his face. Better to lose the battle than the war. She loved what she did, and he certainly wasn't going to ask her to choose. If he continued this relationship, he'd have to get used to interrupted nights and develop a tolerance for cold showers. While she talked, he grabbed his shirt and put it on.

"How long since she came in? And the contractions are irregular? Who's on duty tonight? Dr.

Cashin? Great," Victoria mumbled unhappily, and shook her head.

Dr. Cashin had zero bedside manner. He wasn't a bad doctor, but he was one of the variety that believed in efficient, speedy medicine. No hand-holding, no jokes, no unnecessary conversation.

"Rachel Shelby's a primigravida. Young and worried about labor, according to Wally. She's been having some pretty annoying Braxton-Hicks contractions and some round ligament pain, but he didn't think she was anywhere close to delivering. The cervix was still closed when he saw her a few days ago." She shook her head again. "That's progress since her last visit, but it's still not much dilation. Could even be false labor, given the fact she's early and has a history of Braxton-Hicks. Dr. Cashin wants to admit her? She'd be more comfortable waiting at home until labor settles itself into a regular pattern."

Victoria listened and consulted her watch again. "No, I don't want her released if she lives an hour away either. I'd better come up. I can be there by midnight. No, I don't mind. I'd rather waste a trip than face Wally if I let one of his patients be delivered by C-section for the ever-popular 'failure to progress' or exhaustion. Maybe I can help her settle down so she doesn't wear herself out before active labor hits. Okay. Bye."

When she put the phone down, reality returned and Victoria realized that before she blithely agreed to go to the hospital, she had been about to make love with Joshua. She closed her eyes, and her back stiffened. How awkward could a situation get? What could she say?

Gosh, I was having a delightful time, but I've got to run now and see a woman who's not my patient and proba-bly won't even deliver tonight. But she's scared and a long way from home. So I have to go. And for some strange reason, I feel like I've just been saved by the proverbial bell.

Nothing came out when she turned to face him. She opened her mouth and shut it again.

"It's all right, Vicky. I'll get out gracefully. You don't have to make a speech about how sorry you are." His chuckle was deep and reassuring as he pulled on his boots and tugged his jeans over the tops of them. "Go do your job."

Victoria clutched the afghan more closely to her, wishing she had left a less-revealing blanket at the foot of her bed. "You don't mind?"

"I didn't say that. I said I'd get out and that you didn't have to make a speech."

"Oh."

His shirttail hung over his jeans, and he looked wonderfully rumpled. His body was relaxed, but the muscles in his jaw tightened as his gaze tracked from her toes to her head, making her conscious of the amount of skin peeking through the mesh of the af-ghan. "You do know how to make it difficult on a man though."

Without waiting for a reply, he kissed her on the lips and said, "If you can't find your truck keys, call me. I'll drive you. 'Night, Vicky."

Reflexively, she reached for the chain that normally hung around her neck. She'd taken it off for the dance, since brass clashed with her dress. But she couldn't remember where she'd put it.

Joshua gave her a final hot glance that seared through her, and then he was gone. A few seconds later the motorcycle roared to life, and he drove away just as though nothing unusual had happened. Just as though he hadn't been about to make her lose her mind before the phone call interrupted them.

Joshua Logan wasn't like any of the men she'd ever known. He was a grown-up, Victoria realized. He actually understood that people couldn't always do what they wanted. He understood that she was torn between going and staying.

Empathy was a quality she admired. Many of the midwives with whom she'd trained were known for their ability to feel for others. Some were almost psychic. However, men weren't particularly known for that characteristic. But Joshua was undeniably sensitive to people and their needs. She remembered the teenage girl at the dance, and how he preferred to wait on the porch when she made her home visits.

Thoughtfully, Victoria got dressed, and found her keys. If she wasn't careful, she'd start believing that Joshua was different and worthy of trusting with her emotions.

The night was long and worthwhile. Victoria felt as if someone had taken a sack of oranges and pummeled her, but she didn't care. Rachel Shelby gave birth to a beautiful baby boy at eight-thirty in the morning. Mother and baby were resting fine, and Victoria felt mighty pleased with herself.

Ordinarily, she'd let the mother leave the hospital after about twelve hours, but Rachel had no support system in place at home. Victoria thought she would still be too worn out to drive by herself with a new baby. By mutual agreement they decided that Rachel would stay Saturday night and go home Sunday.

On her way out of the hospital, the chief of staff, William Anderson, hailed her. "Ms. Bennett!"

Although she'd showered and changed, she still felt a bit ragged to be trading barbs with Dr. Anderson. He hadn't been one of the strongest supporters of her presence in the hospital. Tall, thin, and with hair that resembled an ad for Toupees-Are-Us, he held the opinion that malpractice suits were lurking behind every bush, waiting to trap the careless.

"Good morning, Dr. Anderson." *Smile, Victoria.*

"You're not leaving, are you? I mean, your patient just delivered a couple of hours ago."

"And she's fine," Victoria told him in as pleasant a voice as she could manage. She had a mind to send him the latest fact sheets from the American College of Nurse-Midwives. Maybe that would take some of the wind out of his sails. "And so is the baby. The Apgar score was excellent, even though he was a little early."

"Oh. That's good." Anderson frowned. "Very good."

"She specifically told me that the ABC room was

exactly what she wanted," Victoria lied politically. "I think a lot of women in the community are going to appreciate Bodewell's willingness to address their needs."

Anderson perked up. He was as image conscious as the next administrator. "You really think so?"

"Absolutely. Not everyone thinks of birth as a medical procedure."

"That other midwife certainly didn't. Lord, she thought nothing of delivering frank breeches in home settings."

Victoria shifted her bag to the other hand. "You knew the granny-midwife?"

"Yeah. Lara Logan. She's got to be"—he scratched his head—"well over ninety by now."

"Do you know how to get in touch with her?"

Anderson rolled his bottom lip out and shook his head. "No. But you can ask that grandson of hers. Joshua will put you in touch. I've got to get some papers out of my office. I don't usually work Saturdays, you know, but the quarterly budgets won't wait."

Shock roiled through her, stirring up a flash flood of anger. *Joshua!* Feeling shell-shocked, she intoned, "I won't keep you, then."

"You ask Joshua about his grandmother. He'll set you straight." Anderson walked away, leaving Victoria staring at his retreating figure.

Joshua.

He'd lied. *Why?* It was almost as if he were hiding his grandmother from her. He actually denied knowing the granny-midwife when she'd asked him point-blank.

With every step toward her truck, Victoria felt shock being replaced by anger. To think that twelve hours ago she'd almost . . . Victoria tugged the key over her head and wrenched open the door. She'd get some sleep first. She couldn't confront anybody while she was ragged from a protracted labor with an unprepared mother. She needed food, rest, and answers. In that order.

SEVEN

Joshua turned off the country ballad about lying men and cheating hearts. He'd heard about all he wanted to hear on that subject. And since every single song on the radio dial seemed to have the same basic theme, he gave up trying to find a better station. It was almost six o'clock. Victoria had left the hospital before noon, but he hadn't heard a word from her.

Logically, he knew she was probably sleeping, but that didn't make the waiting easier. Restless, he pulled down *Touching History* from the shelves and began to leaf through it, wondering if Victoria had read it. When the book was published, the people in his life had changed. Not all at once, but eventually *what* he was became more important to them than *who* he was. Except to his grandmother. Gran accepted the sight because she had lived with it all her life. The only thing she wanted from him was great-grandchildren.

Everyone else wanted either to crucify him or ride

his coattails. Talk shows loved him. Scientists studied him. Women, who previously thought digging in the dirt was a crashing bore, were suddenly fascinated by the day-to-day activities of an archaeologist; they were equally fascinated by the celebrity attached to a bona fide psychic. Derrick, his agent, had simply kept on doing his job, which was to encourage the hype, field offers, and sell the second book for an obscene amount of money.

Derrick had done his job well. The advance copy of *Ancient Tales—Echoes from the Past* had just arrived in the mail, along with the latest revised, shortened publicity tour proposal which Derrick wanted him to approve. Even on the mountain, life caught up with him. Joshua knew he was going to have to tell Victoria. God, he hated to do that. Sometimes he wished he'd never written the books. Tossing *History* onto the coffee table, Joshua leaned his head back and tried to figure out how to tell her.

Nothing came to mind. Explaining Indiana Jones was going to be a breeze compared to explaining why he'd misled her about his grandmother. Now that he knew her better, he had a feeling that Victoria would have a much easier time dealing with the concept of psychometry and of touching history than with why he thought his grandmother needed protecting from outsiders.

When the noise of a car intruded on his thoughts, he recognized the peculiar creak of the driver's door as it was opened. Victoria had arrived. Joshua wondered how long she'd stay after he told her. Then he wondered how she'd feel about him once the shock and anger wore off.

Most people treated him as if he were not quite sane, or as if he were running a scam. But the people who believed were the worst, because they wanted a piece of his soul; they wanted him to create magic from the past.

Victoria approached the door, reminding herself that she wanted an explanation, not a confrontation. Most of her original anger had dissipated. At least she hoped it had. She'd given herself a million reasons why Joshua might want to protect his grandmother's privacy. A serious illness was at the top of her list of acceptable explanations. At the same time, she cautioned herself against making excuses for Joshua as she had for Richard. A lie was still a lie.

He opened the door before she had a chance to knock. "Boy or girl?"

Their eyes locked immediately, and Victoria knew he'd been waiting for her. Even in the cool autumn night his feet were bare and his gold-colored shirt was untucked and haphazardly buttoned. Strangely, he looked worn out, as if he'd been in a struggle with his conscience and lost. Victoria hoped he'd been feeling guilty about lying to her.

A second or two passed before Victoria curtly answered, "Boy."

Too late, she heard the sharp edge in her voice. She hadn't come here to make pleasant conversation, but neither had she come here to start a fight. Not first thing anyway. Carefully, she adjusted her tone. "May I come in?"

"Sure." Joshua's eyebrows rose as he stepped out of the way. Her body language cued him to keep his distance, but he wasn't certain which of her emotions were generating the signals—nervousness, fear, anger, uncertainty. He pushed mentally, but he couldn't get a peep from her feelings, not a clue. Absurdly, he was once again as much in the dark as someone without his abilities, and he couldn't believe he had to ask the next question. "Is something wrong?"

"You could say that." Victoria strolled past him, purposely controlling her compulsion to blurt out the reason she was there. She wanted him seated squarely across from her and looking directly into her eyes before she asked him why he lied.

"In that case, have a seat," Joshua instructed as he followed her to the living room.

His confession would have to wait until he found out what was bothering her. And so would his need to take up where they left off last night. She was wearing a loose, flowing skirt and one of those oversize sweaters that threatened to slip off her shoulders. Her hair was still a little damp, and he could smell the coconut in her shampoo.

Victoria sat down on the enormous couch and waited to see where Joshua would sit. He chose the other end of the couch, not too close, but not far enough away either. Being near Joshua, even while she was unhappy with him, was unsettling. Especially after last night, after touching his bare skin, after—

"About last night—" Joshua began.

"That's not it," she interrupted, and shook her head firmly. Last night was not a subject she wanted to discuss. Not yet. Not first. Depending on his explanation, maybe never.

"Good." He relaxed and laid his hand along the back of the couch. He didn't want her to regret last night. "I would have called you today, but the hospital said you were there all night. I didn't want to wake you."

"Thanks. It was a long night, and I was really tired this morning." She didn't say anything else, reminding herself not to be fooled by the concern she saw in his expression.

Her mistake with Richard had been wanting to believe he cared about her despite all the evidence to the contrary. She'd learned the hard way that because she wanted to believe something didn't make it true. She needed to understand why Joshua lied about his grandmother before she let her hormones or her heart get any more involved with the man.

"Well . . . are you going to tell me what's wrong?" he asked, seeing the internal struggle reflected in her eyes. "Or do you want me to play twenty questions?"

"I'm having second thoughts," she told him bluntly.

Joshua's brows drew together. "You said this wasn't about last night."

"It isn't," she assured him. "Not directly anyway. It's about whether or not we trust each other."

"Last night we did."

"And last night I didn't know you were lying. Why didn't you tell me, Joshua?" She had the satisfaction of seeing him wince. At least he didn't deny it.

In a split second Joshua's emotions took an unplanned roller-coaster ride. When they settled, he calmly asked, "Who told you?"

Victoria stared at him. "That's all you can say? 'Who told you?' It doesn't matter. Let's just cut to the chase, and you tell me why you tried to keep the truth from me."

An odd half-laugh escaped him. "I thought that part would be obvious."

"Well, not to me! I am not a Gypsy fortune-teller or a mind reader." She tucked her hair behind one ear and flipped it behind her shoulders. "So why don't you explain it to me in very tiny, simple words so I can understand why the man I almost made love to didn't trust me with his past."

"I was going to tell you tonight," he began heavily, knowing that it was a wrong beginning as soon as the words left his mouth.

"Oh, please!" Victoria's hand slapped down on the back of the couch. "And the check is in the mail. How about a little honesty? I thought we were friends, Joshua. We were almost more than friends."

"We are more than friends," he said with a sharpness that dared her to dispute him. "You know it, and I know it. I didn't mean to let it happen, Vicky, but you're the first woman I've cared about in a very long time. You'll have to excuse me if I haven't done everything quite right. I'm a little out of practice."

"Then let me give you a hint. You don't lie to people you care about. You trust them. Even with the bad stuff."

"Hell, Victoria, I didn't lie to you. At least not the way you think. I lied to myself." He got up and paced the room, trying to put his reasons into a coherent explanation. "I thought you knew the first time you came here—*there*—to the old cabin. But then you didn't know anything about me, didn't have any expectations. That's when I lied to myself. I told myself it would be all right to pretend. For a while anyway. I thought, wouldn't it be nice to have a normal conversation again? Wouldn't it be nice to start from scratch?"

"A normal conversation?" echoed Victoria.

"Doesn't sound like much, does it?" Joshua paused behind an armchair and rested his forearms against it, cupping one hand around the other. "I came back to the mountains for the same reason that the original highlanders came here. I wanted some space, and I wanted some solitude. I wasn't looking for friendship, and sure as hell not anything more, but there you were. Bright and shiny and completely uninterested in my past."

The gold ring on his little finger glinted for a second, and a memory flashed through Victoria's mind again, closer this time, buzzing right at the edge of being useful. And then she saw the book on the coffee table.

The memory, the *feeling* of having seen him before, came back in a rush. The bottom fell out of her stomach as she actually felt the color drain from her face. A chill stole up her spine as she looked at the glossy book jacket and caught hold of the memory that had eluded her. The one that had bothered her from the first day she'd seen him. The one that had flirted with her consciousness for so long.

She looked up at Joshua and then down at the photograph on the book, almost in awe. A man's big, powerful hand cupped an ancient ceremonial cup. On the little finger of the man's hand was a gold ring of entwined vines. A familiar ring. Joshua's ring. Joshua's hand.

"Oh, my God," she said quietly. "You really are Joshua Logan."

Cuttingly, he said, "Is it just now hitting you? Is that why you're so calm? Because you realize that I'm famous enough to impress your parents?"

Victoria ignored him, her mouth still open as she absorbed the bombshell that had landed on her.

Watching her, Joshua registered the stunned expression on her face, the tension of her body, and realized she hadn't known. He'd been gearing up to explain about Indiana Jones, and she hadn't even known. She was here only because someone must have told her about Granny Logan.

Damn! He hadn't bothered to put the book away, and now she knew what he'd wanted to explain himself. Uneasily, he waited for the explosion of righteous anger that never came.

For the second time, she ran her eyes over him, over his hands, and stopped at the ring. "The first day I saw you, I rememberered the ring. I couldn't place it, but I remembered it. I remembered your hands, or thought I did. I should have known. I have the book somewhere. In a box."

"If you have the book, why didn't you connect the name?"

"Good Lord, why should I? There's not a picture of you on the book jacket, just your hand. Besides, I wasn't expecting to find you *here*, on the top of a mountain."

"That makes us even. I wasn't expecting to find you either."

"That first day, you held out your hands and asked me what I brought. I didn't understand, but your hands fascinated me. I never connected the two. The memory and you. I can't believe no one mentioned who you were. Wally never said anything."

"Why should he? It's none of his concern. Besides, I've been back for months. I'm old news."

Victoria reached for the heavy book and cradled it on her knees. Gently, she traced the shape of his hand and the chalice on the glossy book jacket. She hadn't thought about these stories in years. "It was incredible, you know. This book. It seemed so real."

"It was real." Joshua's tone was hard, disappointed in her.

Victoria's head jerked up, contrition written on

her face. "I didn't mean it that way. I meant that I could feel the people's emotions, that you made history real. For me. My family has antiques hundreds of years old, but they're not real to me. There's no sense of continuity. No emotion. No story. No family of man. You know?"

He knew all too well, so he simply nodded, stunned that Victoria would understand what he felt when he held those objects in his hands. As if reading his thoughts, Victoria shifted her eyes to the shelves of the bookcase, surveying the museum pieces there.

"I guess that's why I wanted to be a midwife. I wanted to whittle a place of my own in a tiny, obscure corner of history. I wanted to be a part of the link from one generation to the next." A self-deprecating smile formed on Victoria's lips as she put the book back on the coffee table. "Don't say anything. I've already been told that it's a stupid ambition."

"According to whom?"

"Richard."

"I thought you stopped believing in the gospel according to Richard when you divorced him."

Victoria gave him a faint smile. "A declaration of independence didn't free the colonies. It took a war."

"Has he been that hard to forget?"

"Not him. How he made me feel sometimes—dammit, Joshua!" Victoria took a deep breath, composed herself, and hauled the conversation back on track. "This isn't about me. It's about you. About why you kept this from me. About why you lied about your grandmother. At the very least, I think you owe me some answers. And quite possibly an apology."

"I can apologize, but I'm not sure I can explain. Other than to say that I have a hard time trusting people and their motives." He let go of a sigh and pushed away from the chair as she stood up to face him.

"People? Don't you mean outsiders?" she corrected him, paraphrasing from the mountain bible. "You have a hard time trusting outsiders and their motives. Betray you once, and they might betray you again. Or as we flatlanders say, 'Once bitten, twice shy.' Have I got that right?"

"Pretty close," he allowed with a tilt of his head.

"And you thought I might have some sort of hidden agenda, so you didn't tell me."

"I didn't know you then."

"You know me now. You knew me last night. One might even say . . . intimately."

Closing his eyes for a moment, Joshua knew she'd neatly boxed him into a corner. He had to admire her technique—a pinch of guilt, a smidgen of indignation, a hint of humor, and a large dollop of deadly calm. Again he was reminded that Victoria was unique.

She casually folded her arms across her midriff, pushing up the sweater material until the edge fell off her shoulder completely, but she didn't bother to drag it back up. Instead, she waited patiently, searching his face with those solemn gray eyes, being completely and totally *Victoria*.

She hadn't once looked at him as if he needed

psychiatric care. She hadn't shoved anything into his hands and asked him to perform. She hadn't gone starry-eyed with plans for impressing her acquaintances with his notoriety. But then, neither had his friends at first.

When Joshua didn't take the hint, Victoria helpfully suggested, "Why don't you start from the beginning, and I'll tell you when to stop."

He smiled at her suggestion and said, "The beginning was a long time ago."

"I love long stories, and I have plenty of time. As your *friend*, surely I'm entitled to the truth, Joshua."

"Then I suggest you take your truth with a little coffee." He motioned for her to follow him to the kitchen. "I know I could use some."

As he began measuring the aromatic coffee beans into a grinder, he briefly told her about the extensive psi testing in insulated laboratories; about the academic witch hunt that could never disprove his claims but shredded his reputation; about the people who'd used him for his connections and walked away when they didn't need him anymore. He also told her how it felt to hold history in his hands, to see someone's life take shape out of the earth.

By the time he was ready to pour the coffee, he'd gotten to the difficult part, the part he dreaded. The part where he confessed to the voices in his head. He paused to fill two cups and took them to the kitchen island, where Victoria was sitting.

Reaching for the coffee, she declined the cream and asked softly, "How can you give it up? How can you walk away from a career you loved? And don't pretend you don't care, because I can hear it in your voice."

"I gave it up because I didn't have a choice." Joshua warmed his hands on his cup, rolling it slightly between his palms. "I'm at an impasse. I can't go on, and I can't go back."

"What do you mean?"

He looked up. "I took a risk. I stepped off the safe and narrow path and found out too late that it's a jungle out there."

"Out where?"

"Off the mountain. I can't control the emotions anymore. They press in on me, hammering away at my mind like an invasion."

"You hate crowds." Victoria repeated what he'd said in jest several times.

"I hate crowds."

"That's why you came back? Because it was too many people, too many emotions?"

"Yeah. I came back because getting up in the morning was a challenge, because I couldn't concentrate, and the headaches were unbearable. The doctors called it chronic fatigue syndrome for lack of any better diagnosis. It was more like an emotional overload, and the emotions weren't even mine."

He pinned her with a raw gaze. Instead of sympathy or horror, he found hesitation in her eyes. "Go ahead, Victoria. Ask it."

"That's why you did the work on the inside of the house, isn't it?" Victoria remembered her impression of his decorating as tidy, lifeless. "That's why everything is so pristine."

The question caught him off guard. He had expected her to doubt him; instead, she was trying to understand him. "Yeah. Other people's emotions sometimes leave echoes that I can feel, and I didn't want any here. I wanted to start fresh. To see if I could desensitize the part of me that reads emotions. The mountain quiet has helped."

Worry crept into her expression, and she shifted on the stool. "Can you read minds?"

"No." He knew what she was trying to get at. "I can feel emotions, but I don't read thoughts. Not in the way you mean, not words and sentences."

"But you can read emotions," she pressed. "From anyone."

"For the most part."

"From me? Can you read me?" Victoria was horrified at the idea. She never wanted to be that vulnerable again, never wanted to let a man have that much power over her.

Joshua took a swallow from his cup before answering. "No. Not you. You're different somehow. We don't share that connection."

Instead of breathing a sigh of relief, Victoria felt an irrational disappointment. Strangers on the street had a connection with Joshua that she didn't. With her thumbnail she traced the grout between the ceramic tiles covering the island top. "You don't get anything?"

He shook his head. "Not really. Does that bother you?"

"No!" She frowned, hoping she hadn't denied it too quickly. "It just . . . surprises me."

Joshua gave her a look that labeled her a liar. "I doubt that. You work too hard at keeping everything bottled up when you're with me, Vicky."

Running her fingers through her hair in a gesture of resignation, she admitted, "I guess I do. It's a habit. Richard liked to push buttons. He never played fair. Always testing me. He loved to find weaknesses. It was open season on anything I cared about. So I learned to stuff everything beneath the surface."

"I'm still paying for Richard's mistakes, I see."

"Wasn't I paying for everyone else's mistakes?" she shot back, reminding him that she wasn't the only one judging people against past experiences. "When you decided to play Clark Kent and hide your alter ego?"

"Touché."

"Fair is fair. Who do you trust, Joshua?"

Before he answered, Joshua took his cup back to the pot for a refill. "My grandmother." He blew softly across the steaming cup and added, "And I think I'm learning to trust you."

She smiled. "Enough to introduce me to your grandmother?"

"That depends," he told her seriously.

Surprised, Victoria asked, "On what? I already know who you are, so she can't spill the beans."

"It depends on exactly why you want to meet her. I

don't want her treated like a laboratory rat the way I was, or ripped apart for being different. She deserves respect, not curiosity or ridicule. She doesn't deserve to be grilled by the medical establishment."

"The big difference between me and the people who tore you apart is that I'm not trying to make a name for myself!" she snapped at him as she hopped off the stool and crossed the kitchen. When she set her cup in the sink, she added, "And you damn well ought to know that without my having to tell you."

"I think I did. I just wanted to hear you say it."

Victoria froze as she felt the impact of his words like a punch to the gut. *Joshua might be a different man, but she was still being tested, still being asked to prove herself.* Were men genetically incapable of taking a leap of faith? she wondered. Was she asking too much of a relationship to expect a foundation of trust?

Before she could answer that question, her common sense reminded her that if Joshua was testing her, he had more than enough reason to be wary. He'd spent the last few years watching human nature at its worst. Unexpectedly, Victoria felt a twinge of empathy as she realized how much it cost him to meet her halfway when she asked for his help as a guide.

Silently she cursed the part of her that understood Joshua. She didn't want to care about him, but it was too late to walk away. In truth, it had been too late the minute she came up off that cabin bed and saw him standing in the doorway. Her libido controlled the hormones, and the hormones were calling the shots.

They didn't care whether or not Joshua trusted her. They didn't care whether or not her heart got broken.

Victoria knew she was waging a losing battle. The hormones would eventually win, but she was going to do everything she could to delay the final surrender. Besides, he said he was beginning to trust her. Wasn't that a start? He might not have complete faith in her yet, but she could change that. The only question was how to begin.

"Victoria, why are you eyeing me like a used-car buyer assessing my resale potential?"

Snapping out of her thoughts, she couldn't keep an embarrassed smile off her face. "Was I?"

"Yeah, you were. Care to share?"

"No. Are you going to introduce me to your grandmother or not?"

"I guess I'll have to. You haven't left me much choice. Will tomorrow be soon enough?"

"Tomorrow will be perfect. Thank you."

"You're welcome." Joshua watched her as a pregnant silence gathered in the kitchen, creating an awkward tension he couldn't break. All the secrets were on the table, and there was nothing to do but go forward. Unfortunately, the first move had to be Victoria's.

"I should go," she finally said, but she didn't take a step toward the door.

"You *should?*" Joshua raised an eyebrow, setting his cup down in a very deliberate motion, noticing the way her eyes followed his action. "Why should you?"

You have to give trust to get trust, she warned herself. "Honestly?"

"Honestly," he answered as he stood in front of her, hands on his hips.

"Because if I stay," she told him, forcing herself to tell the truth, "then I might be tempted to pick up where we left off."

He ran his index finger inside the neckline of her sweater, teasing the warm flesh. "What's wrong with that?"

"Any number of things," Victoria said, and tried to hold herself very still as he pulled the edge of the sweater lower. "Your grandmother, for one."

Instantly, Joshua's finger stopped exerting pressure, and he stepped away. "What's she got to do with it?"

"You said she was different." Victoria straightened her sweater. "How different?"

"She's . . . perceptive," Joshua conceded.

"*Psychic*'s probably more like it," she told him flatly, and headed for the door. "I would rather not have any fresh intimacies on my conscience when I face her."

Joshua frowned. "Especially not fresh intimacies with her grandson."

"Especially not those."

Walking behind her, he warned softly, "You're eventually going to run out of excuses to avoid the inevitable."

"But not tonight," Victoria whispered, and vanished out the door without a backward glance or even a good-bye kiss.

Joshua let her go, let her feel safe. When she started her car, he closed the door and said, "Won't matter much one way or the other what Gran can see in your soul, Vicky. She can see in mine, and nothing is going to change the fact that you'll be the first woman I've brought home to meet her."

Tomorrow was certainly going to be interesting.

EIGHT

When he telephoned, his grandmother had been delighted by the idea of having a visitor Sunday afternoon. Joshua wished he shared the excitement, but he didn't. Since waking up that morning, he'd felt a nagging uneasiness that wouldn't let go of him. When he pulled into the driveway of Victoria's cabin, the tension inside him settled into a knot in his stomach.

He realized he was waiting for the other shoe to drop; waiting for Victoria to realize she'd made a big mistake last night in so easily accepting what he was; waiting for her to look at him with either speculation or uncertainty. He wondered when he'd begun to care so much for Victoria's opinion.

Before he brought the midnight-blue BMW to a full stop, she appeared at the door of the cabin, gave him an easy smile, and waved. She closed the cabin door behind her and walked out on the porch as he got out of the car. When he couldn't find anything different or missing in her eyes, the tension magically dissolved. He still couldn't read her emotions, but the smile was genuine. Victoria hadn't changed because of what she'd learned last night.

The carefully camouflaged shyness that he found so sexy was still there, lurking beneath the surface. Instinctively, he knew she'd been watching for him, ready to walk out on the porch so she could avoid asking him inside. Not because he was a psychic. Not because he'd omitted a few details of his past. But because the physical tug-of-war going on between them scared the hell out of her. It had taken a midnight motorcycle ride to shake her reserve last time; he wondered what it would take this time.

"I see you got your wheels back," she commented.

"This morning. The mechanic dropped it by on his way to church."

"How convenient," Victoria murmured, wondering if he'd arranged Friday night's jaunt on the motorcycle on purpose.

"I thought so," he agreed, and opened the passenger door for her.

"How far is it to your grandmother's?"

"About twenty minutes," he estimated as he watched her slide into the car, pulling her stocking-covered legs inside much too slowly for his peace of mind. Quietly, he cleared his throat. "You didn't have to dress up."

"Yes, I did. I want to make a good impression." Victoria adjusted the simple but classic dress she wore so that the skirt wouldn't crease from being sat upon.

"Your grandmother had the job before I did. I don't want her to think I am sloppy or dirty."

Joshua shut the door and rounded the car. As he scooted behind the steering wheel, he told her, "Gran doesn't judge people by what they wear." Silently, he added, *She goes a bit deeper than that.*

"Good, because I look like a Sunday school teacher in this," Victoria complained.

"If you're what today's Sunday school teachers are like"—Joshua started the car and put it in gear—"I'm going to have to start going to church again."

"You don't go?" Victoria asked in surprise. He had impressed her as the kind of man who held deep convictions.

"Not for years."

"Not at all?"

Joshua waited a second or two and simply said, "I don't like crowds."

Victoria sucked in a breath and realized her error. The fallout from the highs and lows of people's emotions would have been terrible for him. She stumbled through an apology. "I'm sorry. I didn't mean—"

"No, you didn't." He took his eyes off the road long enough to exchange a brief glance. "So don't worry. Enjoy the scenery instead."

Grateful for his understanding, Victoria stopped agonizing over her blunder and paid attention to the mountains. The trees were beginning the final surrender to autumn, forming a tapestry of evergreen, gold, and deep red. Sycamores splashed a rich yellow-orange onto the canvas of fall; the basswood trees added a shiny bronze. Each day brought more color to the landscape. By the end of the week she knew the views would be spectacular. All she had to do was wait.

As they drove, Victoria confessed, "One of the things I like about the mountains is the sense of order. The sense that everything that should happen will happen—in its own time."

"That's what I'm counting on." Joshua looked sideways at her to be sure she understood the subtext of his remark. She turned her usual shade of pink, and Joshua wondered exactly how much of her turned pink when she blushed.

Victoria chose not to say anything else, letting the conversation drift into a companionable silence. When Joshua turned off the highway onto the road leading to his grandmother's house, Victoria leaned forward in her seat. She felt like a kid about to meet Santa Claus.

Through the trees she could see the large house which was board-sided and unpainted. Shake shingles covered the roof instead of tin, and the porch was nearly covered with plants. It wasn't until they were quite close that Victoria realized the hanging planters were aluminum buckets in various sizes. An old woman with short-cropped white hair stood on the front step to greet them, and her eyes were piercing even from a distance.

Lara Logan stood alone on her porch as the car pulled up the hill, and the couple got out. She drew the shawl more closely around her shoulders and smiled to herself. She could already sense the bond between the two. This young woman had the feel of babies about her, and Joshua's soul felt less burdened than it had in a long time. Finally, she told herself, she had hope of holding a great-grandchild in her arms before being called home. The gift had to be passed on. A fact which J.J. had never accepted.

As the couple walked toward her, she noted the steadying hand J.J. held against the girl's back; the way she accepted his touch as natural. But Lara didn't get the impression they were lovers, which caused her to look askance at J.J. Where were the boy's brains? Surely he didn't intend to let this one slip through his fingers?

"Hello, Gran." Joshua felt her disapproval before he even saw it in her glance, but was at a loss to explain it, especially when his grandmother smiled charmingly at Victoria as he made the introduction. "This is Victoria Bennett. Victoria, this is my grandmother, Lara Logan."

Victoria hesitated a second beneath the sharp, penetrating gaze of the older woman and then extended her hand. "I'm glad to meet you, Mrs. Logan. I've heard a lot about you from the community."

"Nothin' interesting, I'm sure. I'm long past causing good conversation." Lara Logan took her hand and covered it with the other one, patting it companionably. "Everyone calls me Granny Logan, 'cept for J.J. I believe I'd like it if you would too."

"I'd love to."

Lara patted her hand one last time and let go. *J.J. would have to step careful with this one. She wouldn't accept half-measures. For this young woman it would be all or nothing.*

"Both of you, come inside. I've got water on the boil for tea." A hoot owl called in the distance, and Lara shook her head. "Going to be a bad winter, J.J. You be careful on the roads this year."

"Yes, ma'am."

Victoria grabbed hold of Joshua's arm as she passed him, and whispered, "J.J.?"

"Joshua John."

She smiled. "Of course. What else? It's perfect."

Lara's home was as lived-in as Joshua's was sparse. Bits and pieces of her life were everywhere, from the delicate wood carving of a mother and child to the old television topped with the current issue of *TV Guide*.

"Talk amongst yourselves while I get the tea," Lara ordered with a dismissive wave as she slipped her shawl off and disappeared into another room.

Instead of talking, Victoria explored the collection of photographs on an antique credenza protected by a lacy shawl. A very old sepia-toned portrait depicted a well-dressed but stern man and his wife who had a toddler straddling her knee and two other children in their Sunday best beside her. Victoria smiled. None of the children was wearing shoes, and the toddler had an unusually direct gaze that looked a great deal like the one Lara Logan leveled at her earlier.

A picture from the early 1900s featured a handsome coal miner whose strong jaw and mouth reminded her of Joshua's. Judging from the age of the photograph, she decided it was his grandfather. More often than not, however, the photos were of a dark-haired youth, at various ages and possessing only the ghost of a smile, looking directly into the camera.

"Most of these are you," she said.

"Naturally. I'm her only grandchild."

Victoria turned to look at him. "Really?"

"Don't look so surprised. Surely you weren't expecting me to be the seventh son of a seventh son?"

"No, I wasn't," she told him indignantly before she realized he was actually teasing her. Then she smiled ruefully and admitted, "I was expecting another stereotype altogether. I assumed you were one of a passel of young 'uns raised barefoot on the mountain."

Joshua laughed. "Good Lord, I guess you have read all the travel brochures."

"Okay, so I was wrong. But you don't seem like an only child. You're too good at irritating me not to have had some sibling practice."

"Gran would have liked nothing better than to have had a passel, but my grandfather died in a mining accident after my father was born. Dad was an only child, and Gran never remarried. Now there's just me."

Victoria didn't have a chance to say anything else because Granny Logan's footsteps announced her return.

"I made regular tea for you, J.J. Victoria, I have chamomile if you'd like," Lara offered as she walked into the room, carrying a tray with two teapots, one in a Blue Willow pattern and one decorated with dogwood blossoms. Carefully, she set the heavy tray down on the coffee table. "You strike me as the kind of woman who might enjoy chamomile."

"I'd love some," Victoria assured Lara as she watched her pour with a sure and steady hand that belied her age and swollen knuckle joints. "You didn't have to go to the extra trouble though."

"The regular tea's the trouble. I have to stock it special for J.J. Myself, I usually have mint or chamomile. 'Course, now, in the winter, I'm partial to pokeberry juice 'cause it helps my rheumatism."

"Thank you." Victoria accepted the cup from her and sat down in the sturdy rocking chair by the credenza. "I recommend chamomile to my patients on a regular basis. I swear by it actually."

Quickly, Lara looked up from pouring and straight at Joshua. "Patients? Don't tell me you've unbent long enough to socialize with a doctor, of all things?"

"I'm not a doctor," Victoria rushed to explain, wondering what else Joshua had forgotten to mention. "I'm the new midwife in the Triangle."

A slow smile spread over the older woman's face as she handed her grandson his tea. "Well now . . . that explains the babies."

"Babies?" Uncertainly, Victoria looked at Joshua for a cue.

He shrugged.

Lara didn't explain until she poured her tea, sat down in the armchair, and had the first sip. "When you came up to the steps, I thought to myself that you had the feel of babies about you. I've always been partial to babies."

"That's one of the reasons I asked Joshua for an introduction. I understand that you were the lay midwife in this area for quite some time."

"Lord, child, longer than I care to think about." Lara put her feet up on small three-legged stool and adjusted the pillow behind her back. "Nigh onto fifty years. Had to quit because I couldn't get around anymore."

"Rheumatism?"

"No. J.J. finally grew up and went off to college. When he left, I couldn't get around the mountain like I was used to. At night, I can't see my feet at the end of my legs, and the good Lord knows that new babies love the night."

Victoria grinned. "Seems like it. Those are the ones we remember, at any rate. You know, I seem to be providing care to women whom you delivered. Naomi Marlowe, for instance. In fact, she said you attended her mother a number of times."

"Lord yes!" Lara shook her head and sighed. "For a while I counted the seasons by Willie Marlowe. Come fall every year, she had another. Naomi was an easy one. But the last . . . now, that one was touch-and-go for a while."

Stunned, Victoria really hadn't expected the midwife to remember. "Can you recall all of your deliveries that well?"

"No, but Willie had eight in a row. She kind of

stuck in my memory. You'll have 'em that lodge in your memory too. It's unavoidable. If you care about your people." Lara looked at her long and thoughtfully before she said, "And you do."

"Yeah, I do." Victoria was beginning to get used to the piercing looks and the long silences from the older midwife. "I like that connection with my patients. But getting the practice going has been difficult. If it hadn't been for Joshua, I'd still be floundering around, I think."

"What have you got to do with all this, J.J.?"

"Not much, Gran. I'm a glorified chauffeur. That's all."

It was his turn to endure one of her silent inspections. He didn't bother to try to hide his feelings for Victoria, deciding to let his grandmother make of them what she would. He sure as hell wasn't certain exactly what they were beyond a fundamental caring and a physical lust.

Raising her eyebrow, his grandmother turned away and spoke to Victoria. "Well, you certainly couldn't have picked a more experienced man. Lord knows, he rode me around for years," Lara said as she turned to Victoria. "Long before he had his driver's license, he was hauling me over these roads in the dead of night."

Victoria shot a look at Joshua as he leaned comfortably back into the sofa. "Did he drive unconscionably fast then too?"

Laughing, Lara said, "Yes. He always did have a feel for the road though. I never worried a moment when he was driving. 'Course, I was younger then. Not so sure I could take it now."

"I'll remember that the next time you want to go into town," Joshua told her dryly.

Calmly, Lara sipped her tea. "There's a lot of things you'd best remember, Joshua John. Not the least of which is that I still cook your Thanksgiving dinner."

Victoria laughed out loud. Joshua pretended to be chastised. Lara nodded her head in satisfaction and turned her attention to the younger woman. "Where are you from? A voice like that ain't bred in Tennessee."

"Connecticut."

"Then why are you delivering our babies?"

"The Triangle made me an offer I couldn't refuse. They helped me pay for my education."

"In return for what?"

"In return for working here for three years."

"And after that?"

"And after that I won't feel like a weight is hanging over my head."

"You don't plan to leave?" Lara asked, casually swirling the liquid in her cup.

"No."

"There's not much money around here," she warned.

"I've begun to figure that out. But there are other benefits. I've always had an interest in folk medicine and medicinal herbs. It's an expensive hobby in the city, but out here . . . well, I can't wait for spring."

Joshua watched as his grandmother set her cup down and eagerly began an earnest discussion of her favorite remedies and the dried stock she had on hand. Before long they were huddled together on the couch, heads bowed over his grandmother's journal, which was filled with recipes she'd written down over the years. He'd known that Victoria and his grandmother would suit each other. In many ways, they were alike. While they talked, he refilled his cup and quietly enjoyed their pleasure at finding a kindred spirit.

"What do you mean by this?" Victoria asked, and pointed to an entry.

Lara studied it for a moment. "Oh. Claudie Anderson's boy burnt his hand while his mother was down. I always stayed with the families for a day or so after the babies were born. Doing whatever needed to be done. Most times it was catching up the wash and making a meal or two."

"It says here that you 'fixed up his burn.' "

"Wasn't much of a burn. Only took a second. Hardest part was getting him settled down so I could pull the fire out of it."

"What did you use?"

"I like to use a bittersweet salve, but I didn't have any that day, so I used the touch. It wasn't much of a burn. Didn't take no more than a second or two."

Joshua straightened in his chair, waiting for Victoria's reaction. This is what he was afraid of—medicine meeting the unexplained. Accepting psychic abilities in the field of archaeology was a far cry from accepting what most people labeled as faith or psychic healing.

He set his cup down, the chink of it against the saucer rim breaking the quiet.

"Touch?" echoed Victoria. "You have the ability to heal by touch?"

"Not the way J.J. does, but I can do a fair job with burns."

Victoria shot a stunned look at Joshua, who returned her stare, neither admitting nor denying his grandmother's offhand comment. He was testing her again, waiting for a reaction. "Joshua can do it too?"

"You get him to show you sometime."

"Oh, I will," Victoria said, her eyes still on Joshua's. Though his expression was unreadable, his eyes had darkened to a deep blue.

"It's late," he said. "We need to get back."

"He's right," Victoria said, and everyone stood up. She handed her cup to the older woman. "Is it all right if I come back and see you? I don't want to be a pest, but I'd be willing to pay for your time if you'd show me some of what you know about medicinal plants."

Lara smiled and nodded. "I'd like that, but I won't take your money." She raised a brow and looked at Joshua as she said, "Passing on what I know would be a treat."

Kissing her on the cheek, Joshua said good-bye and hurried Victoria to the car. The silence lasted for a scant five seconds.

"Okay, let's start with why you didn't tell your grandmother why I wanted to see her." Even though she had her seat belt on, Victoria managed to turn and wedge herself between seat and door so she could keep an eye on him.

Why hadn't he? Joshua wondered. Simple. He had wanted to see if his grandmother could read her any better, and Gran could. That much had been obvious after the hand-pat on the porch and the baby statement. "I wanted to know if you kept everybody out, or just me. Looks like it's just me."

"What do you mean?"

"What you said about not having any fresh intimacies on your conscience? That was good thinking. I think Gran probably knows more about you than you want known."

"Excuse me?"

"Gran's been rifling through your emotions. Her talent is based on touch too. That hand-patting on the porch? That's pretty much how she camouflages her snooping."

"And you let her!"

"Would you like to tell me how I could have stopped her? You're the one who wanted to talk to her. I didn't exactly drag you up there."

"No, you didn't," she conceded, but with a tiny twinge of lingering resentment.

"If it's any consolation, Gran won't tell me what she knows. She won't even hint about what you're hiding."

"What makes you think I have anything to hide?"

"The eight-foot wall that keeps me out."

"Oh, that."

"Yeah, that. She also likes you. I've never seen her share her journal with anyone."

"It was fascinating," Victoria said. Remembering the journal sparked excitement all over again. "She said she has a couple of books that are older than the one she showed me. I can't even comprehend how much information is crammed on those pages, and she truly doesn't think they're anything special. You know, she was charting deliveries without even knowing she was doing it; noting down which medicinal plants she found to be effective and which were a waste of time."

Joshua negotiated a sharp curve as he murmured, "The two of you looked thick as thieves."

"I could have talked to her for hours. I've never been much of a diarist, but after seeing hers, after seeing all those experiences and emotions jump off the page, I realize that I don't want to forget the details of my life. I don't want my children to forget."

"Gran says, 'We don't bequeath what we collect; we contribute what we create.'"

Softly, Victoria repeated the saying. "What a wonderful way of looking at life. My grandmother, on the other hand, would say, 'The one with the biggest pile of stuff wins.'"

Chuckling, Joshua asked, "And is her pile the biggest yet?"

"Let's just say that she is definitely in the semifinals. She's completely different from your grandmother. How old is Granny Logan? Exactly?"

Joshua did some fast math. He never bothered to keep up with the actual years, mostly because he didn't want to face the reality of all those years adding up. "Ninety-two come January."

"Has she always been able to heal?" Victoria asked, and then realized she'd probably trod on a sensitive area. When Lara Logan confessed to having a healing touch, Joshua's face had done a fair imitation of immovable granite. She doubted he wanted to discuss the subject now, but she'd already broached it. So she hurried to assure him that her interest wasn't idle curiosity.

"The reason I ask is that I've done a little reading about therapeutic touch, and I've seen it used in hospices. It can have such a calming effect as well as reducing the level of pain. I wondered if she learned it or if it was simply something she could always do."

In a flat tone Joshua said, "I don't know. I never asked."

Victoria blinked. "You never asked?"

"We don't discuss the subject."

"The healing?"

"Any of it."

"Why?"

"We don't agree."

"About what?"

"Any of it."

Victoria's eyebrows rose in surprise at his curt answers. Softly, she said, "Your grandmother said you could do it too. The healing."

"But I don't. Now, can we drop this interrogation?" His tone was as effective as a warning siren that the topic was off-limits.

"Okay." After that response she didn't dare ask him anything else about his ability to heal. However, she noted that he said he didn't heal, not that he couldn't. "But I do have to ask one more question."

Joshua sighed, anticipating the worst. "All right."

"Would you mind stopping for dinner? I'm really hungry."

Pleasantly surprised, Joshua agreed, knowing dinner would give him a chance to remind Victoria of the chemistry between them. "What do you have in mind?"

"There's that little hole-in-the-wall place down past Mention."

"Why would you want to go there?" Joshua asked, a little disturbed that her choice felt more like a buddy-date place.

"Last week I saw a tractor parked in front of it. I swear!" She held up her fingers in a Girl Scout oath. "I figure if a guy is so eager for lunch that he won't take the time to get off his tractor and get in his car, then the food has got to be pretty good."

"Good point." Joshua nodded his head in understanding. It wasn't the first time he'd noticed that Victoria took her food seriously. "Katie's Grill it is."

By the time dinner was done and he was standing on Victoria's front porch, Joshua had a whole new appreciation for buddy-dates. He'd discovered they had a way of turning into something unexpected. He'd been out on two real dates with Victoria, and both times all he thought about was her. When he was with her, the world faded away. Like now. He was aware of only the dark night with a quarter moon, the woman in front of him, and the bed behind the door.

"Well . . . good night." Victoria was absently playing with her key, rubbing it between her thumb and index finger. "And thanks for dinner."

Carefully, Joshua took the key, and reached behind her to unlock the door without ever shifting his gaze from her face. "Most women would be scared living out in the middle of nowhere like this. I'd be happy to check and see if any bears have broken in while you've been gone. If you need me, that is."

Victoria cleared her throat. He was too close. All of a sudden the relaxed and laughing friend who'd sat across the table was gone, and in his place was a very sexy man. The intensity that always affected her equilibrium was back in his eyes. She managed to say, "I don't need you. But thank you. I'm sure the bears are all asleep for the winter. I'm probably safe."

"I wouldn't bet on it. Bears don't actually hibernate. They shift gears to a lower speed, but they're still out there, foraging."

"You make it sound like they're ready to gobble me up," Victoria whispered as she stepped backward and bumped into the door, which swung open.

Joshua's hand snaked around her waist and pulled her back. "Maybe they are."

Both of them knew this conversation had nothing to do with bears. Joshua lowered his head and kissed her. He nibbled at her lips, growing more impatient with each touch, but he stopped short of gobbling her up. When he raised his head, he smiled at her. " 'Night, Vicky."

Victoria wrote a few notes and closed the chart with a shake of her head. When Wally had given it to her, he'd been as charming as ever. He truly hadn't seemed to mind that Rachel Shelby wanted to change practitioners. Wonders never ceased, and neither did the passage of time. She could hardly believe it had been two weeks since she'd delivered Rachel's baby.

When Rachel came out of the examination room, Victoria looked up and smiled. "I want to see you again in four weeks. That will be your last postpartum checkup. After that, unless you have a problem, you can return to an annual checkup schedule."

"Can I call you back about scheduling the last checkup?" Rachel put down the baby seat. "I'm in the middle of preparations for the family reunion, and I can barely think right now."

"I'd imagine you barely have time to breathe with a two-week-old infant and a reunion to juggle. How'd that happen?"

"Well, it's a small family and they didn't mind switching the location to here at the last minute. I didn't want to travel with Billy yet, but I really wanted to show him off."

Victoria looked down at the happy baby who lay in the brightly colored baby seat at Rachel's feet. He was gorgeous and hadn't made a peep since Rachel arrived. He opened his eyes occasionally and sighed with contentment.

"He's ready to travel," Victoria assured her.

"Well, I'm not!" Rachel laughed. "I'm just now getting the hang of this mommy stuff. Coming here today was a major event. It took me an hour to organize and get out of the house this morning. As it was, I almost forgot this." She rummaged in Billy's diaper bag and pulled out a flyer. "Here. It's a map and an invitation to the reunion this weekend."

Startled, Victoria took it from her. "Why would you invite me?"

"Are you kidding? You're the guest of honor. Billy's the newest member of the clan, and you delivered him. It's not anything fancy. We're having it on our land. It's more of a picnic. Kids will be running wild, and the adults will pretty much have to fend for themselves. But you'd be welcome. And bring a date, of course."

Victoria didn't quite know what to say. Rachel seemed so earnest and genuine in her invitation. "I'd like to accept, but I never know with my schedule. I've got one patient due a few days after that. Is it okay if I just show up if I can make it?"

"Sure." Rachel picked Billy up, smiling at the baby as if she were struck all over again by what a miracle he was. "I've raved to everyone about how you helped me through this, and Rob would like to say thanks too. Try to come, okay? I know two of my sisters-in-law are dying to meet you. It'd be good for business," she promised.

Unable to resist, Victoria agreed. Once Rachel left, Victoria reached for the oversize purse she carried and fished out the journal she kept with her most of the time now. The bits and pieces of her life were beginning to weave themselves into a tapestry, giving her a feeling of security. Joshua had tried to sneak a peek inside her book the last time he was over, but she'd caught him and whisked it out of his hands, officially notifying him that this was off-limits. He wouldn't talk about healing, and she didn't want to share her journal. Fair was fair. Especially since some of the pages had to do with Joshua and the attraction she spent a lot of energy fighting.

The practice was growing steadily, so she no longer had the excuse of needing all her energies to build it up. Women were knocking on her door now instead of the other way around. Joshua was knocking on her door too, and she was running out of excuses. Their relationship had hit a stalemate. They were beyond friendship but not yet lovers.

Intellectually, she recognized that she was afraid to go further because she was hung up on finding a man that instinctively believed in and trusted her. Regardless of that tidy speech about giving trust to get trust, she was still waiting for Joshua to change the same way she kept waiting for Richard to change.

Maybe it was time she stopped waiting and just plunged right in.

"Explain to me again why we're going to this shin-dig?" Joshua teased her as they got out of her Range Rover, which, in a fit of generosity, she had allowed him to drive for once.

"We are here," Victoria explained, shoving her arms into a blue-jean jacket, "so I can bask in the glory of having delivered the newest member of this family."

"Oh?" Joshua commented, and grabbed her hand to pull her back as she started toward the throng of people gathered by the river's edge. "I thought you didn't care about glory."

"This is different. It's not really my glory. It's Rachel's glory. I just get to share."

"Sharing. Isn't that where you play with her toys and she can't complain when you break them?"

"Something like that." Victoria smiled. She could get used to the quiet, gentle teasing of Joshua Logan.

He ran a finger down the bridge of her nose and over her lips to her chin. "It isn't fair for you to look like this in public. The nip in the air has made your cheeks pink. Your lips are incredible, and you look about eighteen with your hair in that ponytail. I feel like I'm robbing the cradle."

Victoria laughed and eyed him critically. He wore a flannel shirt open at the neck with a wheat-colored T-shirt beneath, loose-fitting jeans, and expensive leather sneakers. "Six years' difference is not robbing the cradle. You don't look old. Except for maybe that tiny bit of gray at the temples. And the worry you get around your eyes when you have to meet a crowd of people. They don't bite you know."

"Not when I'm around you," Joshua told her seriously. "I'm so damn busy wanting you that I tend to ignore all the other signals."

NINE

Now the pink in her cheeks was caused by more than the cool autumn weather. Not knowing how to answer the raw hunger in his eyes, at least not in public, Victoria looked away and led him down the hill. A half-dozen picnic tables were scattered around, and two grills were fired up, cooking hot dogs and hamburgers. Ice chests full of sodas and beer were opening and closing at an alarming rate.

Rachel saw them first, grinned widely, and waved with her whole arm. She grabbed a good-looking young man by the arm and dragged him over. "You made it! This is Rob."

He extended his hand. "Thanks for coming. I didn't know how much this community needed you until Rachel told me what would have happened to her if you hadn't been there. I didn't want her to go through that alone in a room with no one to sit with her. If I'd had any idea the baby was coming early—"

"Don't beat yourself up," Victoria interrupted with a laugh. "Babies come when they darn well please."

That answer seemed to relieve him, as if he'd been waiting for her to chastise him for being out of town. Then he turned to Joshua and held out his hand again. "Hi, I'm Rob Shelby."

After a fraction of second Joshua held out his hand to complete the handshake. "Joshua Logan."

Victoria noted that the gesture was extremely brief despite the friendly smile that never faltered. For the first time, she realized how good Joshua was at hiding his reactions to the people around him. She also knew that he had come only because she asked him. Somehow it meant a lot to her that Joshua would put himself in what might be an uncomfortable situation simply because she had asked it of him.

"Aren't you—" Rob began as recognition flickered in his eyes.

"Yeah," Joshua answered, and got hit squarely in the back with a football before he could say another word. He staggered slightly and made a sound faintly like *ooof*.

Three preadolescent boys came racing toward them, bumping into each other as the first one caught a glimpse of Joshua's face and stopped on a dime. Victoria was reminded of the Three Stooges, but she hid her smile.

Rachel coughed and said with a glint of mischief in her eyes, "These are our nephews. Larry, Moe, and Curly."

Unable to stop herself, Victoria burst out laughing, and so did the men. The youngsters exchanged puzzled glances, not quite sure what the grown-ups found so funny. The first one spoke up. "Those aren't really our names, mister. We're sorry about the football. It was an accident."

Joshua calmly picked up the ball at his feet and said, "Go long."

It took the kids only a second to comprehend that the man wasn't angry and to scramble out into the pasture. Joshua let them get some distance and then he drilled a pass to the one on the far left. In that split second the boys' expressions changed from uncertainty to adoration. Obviously, here was an adult worthy of respect.

To Victoria's surprise, a few minutes later they had Joshua involved in a lively touch football game as she alternately refereed and talked to people that Rachel introduced. Watching Joshua handle the boys so naturally brought back some old longings she thought were banished for good. The sight of Joshua tussling on the ground with kids and the atmosphere of the family reunion made her remember that she wanted more in her life than her parents had had in theirs.

She'd always hoped for the picket-fence ideal. She had wanted to watch her own loving husband and children mix it up on the lawn. She'd wanted to live in a house that echoed with life and laughter. When she divorced Richard, she'd given up on that dream and managed to forget or ignore those longings. Until she'd moved to Tennessee. Now Joshua was making her want those things again.

Finally exhausted, Joshua begged off from the game, which had grown to about ten people, and joined Victoria on the sidelines. His shirt was unbuttoned, revealing the T-shirt beneath, and his hair was a bit damp from the exertion. As he dropped to sit on the ground beside her, he said, "You didn't tell me I should have been working out for this."

Victoria curled her fingers to keep from reaching out and laying a hand on his chest to feel the heat she knew was there. "Who knew you would want to toss a pigskin around? Besides, I wouldn't worry about your shape."

"Really?" Joshua teased, fishing for a compliment.

"No, I think it was your strategy that lost the game, not your conditioning." Victoria widened her eyes and cultivated a serious but innocent expression. "I have a few suggestions that might help next time."

Joshua gave her an offended huff. "Next time, *you* get in the game and then maybe I'll listen."

"Next time, maybe I will. I'm pretty good at catching passes."

"Not so you'd notice," Joshua said dryly. "You're much better at deflecting them."

Victoria ignored him and changed the subject. "Have you noticed the way children respond to you?"

"Not particularly."

"Well, they do. In fact, you seem more comfortable with the kids than the adults," she said quietly. "Are they easier for you?"

Joshua didn't pretend to misunderstand her. Since the meeting with his grandmother, he'd given up trying to hide anything from Victoria. "With well-adjusted kids like these . . . yeah, it's easier. They don't want anything from me except some attention. Their emotions are clean, no murky depths to suck me under and make me worry about things I have no power to change. The biggest issue they're dealing with is whether or not to confess to breaking the front door glass."

"Did one of them actually do that?" she asked.

"Curly."

"Wait a minute. You don't read minds!"

"Of course not. Curly let something slip and then made a show of asking me in confidence what my opinion was, considering I'm way-cool for an adult-type person."

"Oh, please!" Victoria tried to give him a hard nudge with her elbow in an attempt to deflate his ego, but he scooted away before she connected. "What did you tell him?"

Joshua stood up and looked at the group of children, who were now busily making human pyramids, and said, "Way-cool types always recommend honesty as the best policy. Let's get something to eat."

Taking his hand, she let him pull her to her feet, but she hung back when he started toward the grills. She took the plunge she'd been thinking about for so long. "Would it hurt your way-cool image if we skipped the picnic and went back to my place for dinner? I feel like cooking all of a sudden. Something a little more substantial than hot dogs and chips."

"Love, you can heat up anything you want. All you have to do is tell me when."

Victoria swallowed. "You'll probably want a shower."

He nodded. "Probably."

"So why don't I drop you at your house and you can come by after that?"

"Why don't we say good-bye to our hosts?" he asked, and wasted no time flagging down Rachel and Rob.

Joshua huddled deeper into his jacket to ward off the dropping temperatures of the early November night. Warmth was only a few feet away, but he sat in his car for a moment before going up to Victoria's door. They'd been in and out of each other's company for weeks. He knew her well enough to realize that this was more than an impromptu dinner invitation. This was an invitation into Victoria's life.

He'd already invited her into his. She'd met his grandmother. She knew all his secrets. Now she was symbolically returning the favor. Joshua knew beyond a shadow of a doubt that he was going to make love to Victoria that night. More than anything, he wanted her to drop the walls. For the first time in his life he actually wanted a complete emotional and physical bond. He wanted to be as much a part of Victoria as she was of him.

Surrendering to the inevitable, he faced the fact that he'd gone way past lust without ever realizing it. He'd fallen in love with his new best friend and his tenant. And unless he was mistaken, Victoria had fallen in love with him.

Neither one of them had been looking for love. Neither one of them had really believed in love. Even if he had, he couldn't have chosen a worse candidate than Victoria. She was a medical professional from a background that rewarded fame and glory. Because of her training, she should have been skeptical of his abilities; because of her parents, she should have been trying to figure out how to use him or use his connections. Instead, she accepted him without question and hadn't once asked for a "little" favor of any kind.

Well, she had asked for an introduction to his grandmother, but she could have gotten that without him. And what she was taking from Gran was something that his grandmother desperately wanted to give —some of her wisdom, her life's work. Gran was a big believer in tradition, in passing life's wisdom from generation to generation.

Gran felt she'd failed with him because he'd never wanted any part of the sight until he held that first stone cup. Now he wanted to distance himself from his ability again, and she was back to being disappointed. Only this time her disappointment was laced with an urgency that hadn't been there before.

The porch light flicked on and interrupted Joshua's thoughts. Victoria knew he was there and was politely telling him to get inside. Climbing out of the car, he admitted to himself that the reserve and tact she displayed on the surface intrigued him as much as the passion he knew was simmering beneath the surface.

Victoria opened the door as soon as he knocked. She had one hand on the doorknob and held a ladle in the other. A dish towel was thrown over her shoulder, and she wore the tropical reef T-shirt she'd had on the first day he met her, except she didn't have a bra on. He could see the ripe swell of her breasts as the cotton molded around them.

"Spaghetti had better be one of your favorite foods," she said without preamble. "This recipe will feed a family of twenty."

"I can do some damage with a fork and a spoon."

She grinned. "Good, because I don't chop up my spaghetti. It's twirl or starve around my house."

Victoria reached for Joshua's plate. They finished dinner half an hour before, but they hadn't managed to get away from the table. "I guess I'd better get these dishes washed."

"I can help," Joshua volunteered, and pushed his chair back. "It's one of my few domestic skills."

"Sit!" ordered Victoria. "I don't know how they do this in your family, but in mine the guest never washes dishes. Of course, neither does the host, but that's beside the point."

Joshua studied her as she turned her back and began to fill a sink with water. "Do you miss it?"

"Miss what?" asked Victoria as she slanted a glance over her shoulder.

"The life-style."

Victoria scraped the plates as she considered the question. It wasn't the life-style she missed so much as her parents' approval. Carefully, Victoria slipped the dishes into the soapy water, and returned to the table to collect the salad bowls and glasses. "I miss being the perfect daughter."

He guessed, "You did something you *shouldn't* have done."

"Yeah."

"You *should* have gone home and not to Tennessee."

"Right." Victoria walked the few steps back to the sink and put the rest of the dishes in to soak. "My parents love me, but they aren't quite sure how to treat me now that I've broken the mold. In their book, being happy doesn't count in the perfect-daughter sweepstakes because they have never understood how I could have been unhappy in the first place. Being good at what I do doesn't count toward being the perfect daughter either, because what I am doesn't fit their definition of success."

"Money, fame, and glory," Joshua murmured under his breath, but she heard him.

"Right," Victoria said, and tried to lighten the mood. "And none of those three are connected with the world's second oldest profession."

Joshua joined her by the sink, putting the salt and

pepper shakers on top of the bread box at the far end of the counter. "Second oldest profession?"

"Sure. Midwifery is sort of a spinoff from the world's oldest profession. We came along about nine months later."

He chuckled. "I never thought of it that way."

She turned and reached for the spaghetti pot, intending to pour out the water she'd left in it to soak, but as soon as her palms touched the sides of the kettle-type pan, she knew she'd made a mistake. Hot metal seared her skin, and she instantly snatched her hands away with a loud, anguished curse. Closing her eyes, she willed the fire in her palms to go away, but even before examining them, she knew that was impossible. Thank God she hadn't actually picked it up.

When she opened her eyes, Joshua was right beside her, pulling her to the double sink. He twisted the cold water tap and grabbed both arms by the wrists, shoving them beneath the soothing stream of cold water.

"Keep them there," he ordered.

"Don't worry," Victoria assured him in a strained voice. "Check the stove. I must not have turned off that electric eye all the way."

He reached over and jiggled one of the four stove knobs. "You're right. You didn't. It's barely on, but enough to heat that pot of water."

Victoria bit her lip as she finally pulled her hands out of the water and looked at them for a second before the throbbing crescendoed again. "Looks like more of a light scorch than a blistering burn." She immediately returned them to the comfort of the cold and asked, "Why do burns have to hurt so much?"

"Maybe Mother Nature doesn't like having to make the same point twice," Joshua told her as he leaned over her shoulder. "Let me see."

"I already told you. It's a scorch, and it's going to hurt for a bit. Check the living room windowsill. I've got an aloe vera plant."

"Let me see your hands," Joshua repeated, and this time the command in his voice was unmistakable.

"The aloe vera—" Victoria began, and then stopped. Slowly she brought one hand out of the water stream and turned to Joshua. He cradled the back of her hand in his palm, his thumb rubbing softly against the outside line of hers.

"You're going to have to trust me." It was a statement, not a plea. "You wanted to know about this. Now, shut up about the plant and let me take the fire away. Think of something good."

Mesmerized by the quiet confidence in his manner, Victoria managed only a slight nod. The throbbing in her hand had begun again. If he didn't make the hurt go away soon, she'd have to put it back under the water. Victoria closed her eyes and tried to think of something besides the hurting in her hand. Something that felt good.

Joshua took his free hand and gently covered Victoria's palm, cocooning her hand inside his. He concentrated on feeling the pain and let his fingers softly massage the tender pulse point of her wrist. For him, when he made the connection, finding her pain was like suddenly falling through the floor. He had to scramble to catch himself.

She was right, it was just a scorch, but an acute one. Slowly he accepted the pain and began to wash it away with gentle strokes that hovered above her skin but never touched her. With each sweep he slid deeper into sync with Victoria.

When he reached for her second hand he noticed that she didn't even open her eyes. He repeated the process of touching and accepting her hurt, only this time when he made the last stroke, the pain was replaced with pleasure—a bolt of sensual pleasure so strong that Joshua actually felt himself harden in response.

Victoria's feelings were all of him, a jumble of impressions from the night they'd almost made love and of new scenes that held him in thrall. Gone was the shyness, and in its place was confidence and desire. He could sense darkness illuminated by the glow of candlelight. He could feel the satisfaction she got from knowing he was excited by the sight of her as she stripped slowly in front of him.

Forcing himself to pull away, Joshua knew he'd seen erotic fantasies that he was never meant to see. This was what Victoria was afraid of revealing—how much she wanted him and how deeply she felt the physical attraction between them. There was no mistaking the intensity of her emotions. He could think of only one reason that would have prevented her from acting on her impulses. She had been afraid of pursuing a relationship because she wasn't sure she could handle disappointment again.

Since he hadn't made any secret of his desire for her, Joshua realized that she wasn't afraid he'd reject her physically. She was afraid he'd reject her emotionally. Considering her first marriage, Joshua knew how scary that rejection would be to Victoria. She'd learned to keep herself safe.

How ironic that the one woman from whom he wanted emotion had learned how to turn it off and on. Didn't she know he wouldn't turn away from her? Didn't she trust him yet?

Without releasing her hand, Joshua turned off the tap. Slowly, she opened her eyes and cautiously flexed her hands, testing for any lingering pain.

Stunned, Victoria stared at her palms. Skin which had been a bright pink was now flesh-colored again. Hesitantly, she curled her fingers and waited for the telltale throbbing of tissue still protesting the burn. Opening her fingers again, she rubbed one palm with the fingertips of her other hand and then reversed the process. The skin seemed more sensitive than usual, but that was the only sign of injury.

"This is the most amazing thing I've ever seen," she whispered. "I know I grabbed that pot. My hands were burned. I saw them. I *felt* them. Do you know what you just did?"

She looked up. Joshua stood silent, leaning against the edge of the counter with his arms crossed over his chest. His expression was guarded, not at all like someone who'd just performed a minor miracle.

Granny Logan had told her that Joshua fought himself and his gift. Always had.

"Why does offering a kindness to a friend make you so uncomfortable?" she wondered aloud. "Why do your abilities make you so uncomfortable? Your grandmother calls it a gift. And believe me—it is!"

He laughed hollowly. "Well, it's not a gift I wanted. I didn't ask for it. And when I used it, it screwed up my life."

"What do you mean?"

"I've got plenty of money, but I lost my career." Joshua pushed away from the counter. "I can't finish a site anymore. It gets too personal. I lose my focus and my concentration. Emotions crowd in on top of me."

"I thought you were getting better."

"Oh, I am," he assured her. "But I'm *here*, on the mountain. I'm not trying to touch history. I'm not out there jostling through crowds buying Christmas presents or trying to dig up bits and pieces of someone else's life."

"Then what are you trying to do?" she asked softly.

Joshua leveled a steady gaze at her. "I'm spending a lot of time trying to convince you that we need to be together."

"What happens after you convince me?" Victoria asked quietly, uncertain what she wanted his answer to be.

"I won't have to be alone anymore."

His response stopped her cold. From the beginning she'd thought of him as the strong, silent type who was at peace with his solitary existence. She'd never once thought of him as lonely. Everything he did, he did by choice. Until now she hadn't realized it was a bitter choice. "Joshua, I didn't . . . I thought . . ."

He caught her arm right above her elbow and drew her closer, running his hands up over her shoulders and down her back. When he pulled her into his embrace, he promised, "You can trust me, Vicky. Let me love you."

For the moment, his words were enough for Victoria. She wanted to trust him. She wanted to love him back. She wanted to heal his hurt the same way he'd healed hers—by touch. Rising on her toes, Victoria circled her arms around his neck and pulled his head down to meet her lips. "I've made a decision. The dishes can wait, but I can't."

There was no hesitation or exploration in his kiss. It was pure possession. His hands crept lower, cupped her rump, and raised her up until she was half sitting on the table with him between her legs, his arousal pressed intimately against her. When she hooked a leg around his thigh, he stilled for a moment, breaking the kiss and resting his forehead on hers.

With a suddenness that took her breath away, he snatched her off the table and carried her to the bed. As Victoria fell back into the softness, he stepped away and caught her ankle. Slowly he pulled off her shoes one at a time and dropped them to the ground.

"I've wanted to take you in this bed since the first day I saw you lying on it. When you stretched and arched your back, I truly thought I'd died and gone to heaven."

Victoria colored at the memory.

"And then you blushed, and I wanted to know how much of you turned pink." Joshua stripped his sweater off and tossed it over the footboard. "Take the shirt off, love."

Shyly at first, Victoria eased up off the mattress, caught the bottom of the T-shirt with her hands, and pulled it over her head in one smooth movement. She laid her arms across her midriff, unconsciously pushing her breasts up and creating an enticing valley of shadow.

"You take my breath away, Victoria. Do you know that? Do you understand what you do to me?"

"Yes," she whispered. "Because you do the same thing to me."

She reached out then and flattened her palms against his rib cage. He sucked in a breath but let her explore. Her fingers splayed out as her hands moved upward, her fingertips brushing his nipples. She could feel him tense beneath her touch, and she smiled. Neither one of them was in control, and that was how it should be.

This was what he meant when he'd asked her what she knew about lust, sex. And he'd been right; she hadn't known nearly enough. All of this was new to her. Before, she'd always been afraid to ask for what she wanted, but tonight she didn't even bother to ask. She just took. She wanted Joshua to know that she was his. She wanted him to know that she wanted them to be together as much as he did.

The warmth beneath her hands contrasted sharply with the slight chill in the cabin. She felt her nipples pebble from the combination of excitement and cool air. But she didn't want to cover up. Judging from the restrained hunger blazing in Joshua's eyes, he didn't want her covered either.

A half-smile hovered on her lips as she retraced the path her fingers had taken and dipped lower to unfasten his pants. She was fascinated by the thin, dark line of hair that disappeared beneath his waistband, only to reappear as she opened his trousers and began to push his clothes down his hips to expose his flat, tensed abdomen.

Joshua had given up breathing the moment her fingers toyed with the edge of his pants. The muscles in his stomach tightened and his arousal jerked when the sliver of anticipation coursed through him. By the time she freed his shaft, his head was tilted back and he'd closed his eyes. In order to maintain any control at all, he couldn't watch. One glimpse of her hands on him, stroking him . . .

"Enough," Joshua said in a rasp and caught her hands, which was a mistake.

In catching her hands, he closed them over his arousal and drew them upward, which only intensified the shudder of pleasure that threatened to grip him. Breathing deeply now, Joshua kicked off his shoes, fished a foil packet out of his pocket, and finished disrobing. When he was through, he turned his attention to Victoria and leaned over her, one knee beside her thigh on the bed.

"Your turn," he said, and grasped the waistband of her stretch pants, peeling them off her, which left only her panties between them and consummation. When Victoria's hand strayed toward the waistband, he pushed it away. "Not yet. I don't want any temptation until I've protected you."

Victoria's hips rocked slightly in frustration. This dance between them had gone on long enough. She wanted him inside her. She wanted to feel his strength and power as he took her.

Slowly, he shifted her on the bed and drew her arms up over her head, holding them easily with one big hand. With the other he teased her, rubbed her through the silky fabric covering her mound. Victoria's legs parted in a silent signal for him to explore further, to satisfy the pulsing that had begun in the heart of her desire.

Simultaneously, he sucked a nipple into his mouth and slid his hand beneath her panties, spreading her petals with his fingers. Victoria gasped, incapable of words. She tried to urge him on with the motions of her body, but she seemed incapable of doing more than reveling in the sensations that Joshua created so easily with his tongue and fingers. And then he entered her with his finger, teasing her with his thumb. Victoria's eyelids fluttered closed as she gave herself up, knowing there was nothing she could do to stop Joshua from taking his time.

When Joshua felt her surrender to the moment, he

removed her panties and sheathed himself. As he knelt over her, she opened her eyes, and he knew, at this moment, she was vulnerable. That her emotions were his. Everything she had was his. He reached between them to guide his arousal, holding back from taking her in one long, deep stroke.

She was wet, ready for him, but he wanted her to regain that peak, the edge she'd almost tumbled over. He let her hold him in her passage, and he circled the sensitive nub of flesh with the pad of his thumb. With each stroke she drew a little closer to that precipice, and he drove a little deeper.

Soon, each touch was eliciting a ragged gasp of air from Victoria. Joshua could feel his own climax building, enhanced and spurred on by the pleasure beginning to ripple through her. When she breathed his name, she got out only "Josh," but she said it again and again as pleasure burst inside her and spiraled through her. Joshua shifted his hands to her hips, pulling her to him one last time and felt not only his climax but hers as well. For the first time, Victoria's emotions spilled over into him, uncensored.

Neither of them had the inclination or the energy to talk for a while. Joshua got out of bed long enough to stoke the wood stove and turn out the lights, and then joined her on the old mattress that remembered the shape of his body and accepted him as though he'd never moved away.

Joshua woke to darkness and embraced the night. He'd always loved the night. It was silent. As he lay there, his eyes grew accustomed to the blackness, and he turned his head to watch Victoria. She was sleeping between him and the wall, on her back, and with both arms thrown over her head. Dark hair spilled across her pillow and onto his. He didn't mind.

While she slept he could feel that calmness, that balance that she possessed. And yet when he made love to her, he could feel the passion. His brows drew together. He felt closer to her, but the barriers were still up. Maybe they always would be.

She stirred and rubbed the tip of her nose. Sleepily, she yawned and asked, "Why are you staring at me?"

"I wasn't staring," he said, and adjusted to fit her body next to his side. "I was enjoying the view."

"The view's better in the daylight with fresh makeup," she told him prosaically.

"I like it just fine."

"Go to sleep, Joshua."

It was good advice, and he took it.

Victoria knew her life had changed before she opened her eyes. The first clue was the steady rise and fall of her head which was pillowed on Joshua's warm, hard chest. The second clue were his legs all tangled up with hers. But the last and best clue was the feeling of being whole for the first time in a long time.

Extricating herself was going to prove too difficult

to do without waking up Joshua, so she didn't bother to try. She lifted her head and kissed him on the lips.

"Good morning," she greeted him cheerfully.

Joshua cracked an eyelid, took a deep breath, and closed his eye again.

She smiled. "Someone's been sleeping in my bed."

He opened an eye again.

"And he's still here," she whispered.

"You sound happy."

"I am."

"No morning-after second-guessing?"

"No. And no complaints either."

Joshua managed to look offended. "I should sure as hell hope not!" Then he grinned devilishly. "Of course, the second time was technically more successful. I don't recall ever having tried that position."

When Victoria blushed, he decided to make a habit of lazy Sundays in bed.

Lara Logan noticed the change in Victoria as soon as she stepped through the doorway and slid out of her coat. The sense of babies was still there, but fainter. As though something else in her life had risen to the top of her awareness in the past couple of weeks. Something like a partnership. All that internal agonizing had finally resolved itself. And Lara had a pretty good idea how the conflict got resolved. Just the same, she gave the younger woman a comforting pat on the shoulder as she ushered her inside for their weekly cup of tea.

The touch told her everything she wanted to know. Barring unforeseen circumstances, it was only a matter of time before she held her great-grandchild. Unfortunately, she was getting a little short on time, and even with the sight, she couldn't predict the unpredictable. Still, all in all, she had hope again.

"Joshua tells me that you aren't going home for Thanksgiving," said Lara.

"Not this year."

"You can eat here, you know. It's not fancy, but it's a turkey."

"I'd like that."

"So would Joshua," Lara told her, and gave a satisfied nod of her head before she reached for the teapot.

"Is the coast clear?" Joshua asked as he stuck his head inside Victoria's office.

Looking up from her journal, Victoria smiled. She hadn't actually admitted it to him yet, but she was in love. "Yep. You're safe. My last patient canceled, so I caught up my paperwork."

"Good." Solemnly, Joshua walked over to the table in the corner and handed her a shiny brass key.

Surprised, she took it and said, "What's this?"

"A key."

"Thank you. I can see that. What does it unlock?"

"My house."

Victoria laughed. "What do I need a key for? You hardly ever lock your house."

"It's symbolic," he told her with a crooked smile.

She stared at the key, knowing it represented progress in the trust department. He hadn't come all the way yet, but he was trying. "Thank you. I love it."

Under his watchful eye she added his door key to the car key on her necklace.

Victoria was cursing as she roared up in Joshua's driveway. The only thing he'd ever asked her to do was help him entertain his agent, who insisted on visiting to talk about promotion on the new book. The only thing Joshua had asked of her—and she had to be running late.

Sighing with relief, she saw that only Joshua's car sat in front of the house, which meant the agent hadn't come early. As quickly as she could, she braked to a stop and killed the engine. One glance at her watch warned her that she had a scant twenty minutes to shower and change.

By the time she'd gotten in the front door, she was thanking her common sense for prodding her to put her clothes and a bag of cosmetics in the truck that morning—just in case—so she wouldn't have to go home. She swung through the living room on the way to the back of the house and dropped her purse by the couch. "Joshua!"

"Yeah," he called from the back of the house.

She started for his voice. "I'm late."

"I noticed," he assured her as he came down the hall toward her. He had on gray slacks and a bulky knit sweater the color of the winter sea on Cape Cod.

"Oh, thank God, you're dressed. I need the shower and your bathroom mirror."

"You look fine."

Victoria gave him a dirty look. "Fine is not a word you want to use to a woman about to meet your agent."

"What's all the fuss?"

Clenching her teeth, she forced air out in a strangled sound as she passed him. "I'd like to make a good impression."

"You weren't this way about meeting my grandmother, and you wanted to make a good impression."

"I dressed for her out of respect, not because I thought she'd size me up and dismiss me based on my image."

Joshua reply was very soft. "Neither will Derrick. I'm not Richard, love. I don't care whether or not you impress the people I know."

If she heard him, his words didn't seem to register. She stopped in the bedroom doorway, tapping her forehead with the heel of her hand. "Would you get me those silver dolphin earrings in the bottom of my purse? The dangling ones I bought last week? Thanks."

Joshua watched her disappear into the bedroom.

A quick search of the house yielded the location of the suitcase she called a purse. Joshua hoisted it onto the coffee table, wondering if this quest was going to be like looking for a needle in a haystack. With trepidation, he unzipped it.

TEN

Her journal was on top, which made rummaging impossible. Joshua lifted out the book, resisting the urge to peek inside. It was a clothbound volume that looked more like a book of poetry than a journal. A red satin ribbon was attached to the spine as a marker. Just like Victoria, her possessions rarely yielded impressions as he handled them. He set it on the table and looked back in the purse.

Now that he had room to work, he angled the purse opening toward the light and started shifting things with his hand. He found a wallet-sized photo album, a Magic Marker, four paper clips, spare change, cash register receipts, assorted pens and pencils, loose change, cinnamon candies, and a mink checkbook cover, no doubt left over from Connecticut days. Something lustrous and square was wedged in a crease at the corner, so he fished around and caught hold of the object.

As soon as he did, he fell into a moment of the past. The emotions inside the object caught him, urging him along until he settled into the rhythm of the moment. He hovered above and yet inside Victoria as the scene played out. The split consciousness was as familiar to him as breathing.

She was young—fourteen maybe—and standing in the center of a gazebo. Joshua felt her crushing unhappiness before he felt the first tear. When she opened the object in her hand and lifted it to eye level, he realized it was a fancy gold compact with mirror. The face he saw was solemn, one tear streaking down toward the corner of her mouth. She reached out and caught it with the tip of her tongue. She wanted a new face, Joshua knew that as well as he knew his own name. When she spoke, it was in a whisper.

Mirror, mirror, in my hand, who's the fairest in the land? Not me. Never me. Powdering my nose in a gold compact isn't going to make me pretty.

Caught in the never-never land between child and woman, she couldn't see what those around her saw. She couldn't see the promise of beauty in eyes too large for her face or in the rich darkness of her hair. Her birthday gift was such a disappointment, it had been all she could do to act delighted and then slip away to cry.

Suddenly, Victoria snapped the compact shut and put it in the pocket of her shorts, which looked too short for the long legs poking out beneath them. Drawing in a breath and expelling it in a deep sigh,

Victoria headed back to the house, hiding her emotions again.

As she walked away, the feelings faded, and Joshua was left holding the engraved metal compact. He turned it over and read the inscription, wincing as he did. "To my very own funny-face with love, Daddy."

"Wrong choice of words, pal," Joshua whispered. "If you only knew."

Then his hands tightened on the compact. This time the rush of feelings he got was his own. He'd finally gotten an emotional impression of Victoria, albeit it secondhand. He finally had a piece of a connection. It wasn't much, but it was a start.

Giving up on the earrings, he let everything slide out of his hands and back down in the purse, which he picked up and carried with him to the bedroom. He rapped on the bathroom door. When he heard her turn off the shower, he said, "Victoria, I can't find the earrings, so I brought your purse to you."

"I could have sworn I put them in there," Victoria griped as she came out of the bathroom wrapped in a towel. Her hair was twisted into a bun on top of her head and held up by nothing more than a pencil.

"How'd you do that?" Joshua asked, and deftly pulled the pencil free.

Victoria's hair came tumbling down, and she combed it with her fingers. "Trade secret." She plucked her purse out of his hands. "I'll be ready in five."

"Right," he said with skepticism.

"Okay, it'll be more like ten minutes."

"Well, I can't wait that long." His voice was deep and his tone final. He kissed her, slow and thoroughly. Pulling the towel away, he let his hands roam over soft, supple skin which was still damp from the shower. When he broke the kiss, he handed her the towel and raised an eyebrow, giving her a choice.

Victoria read his intent from the desire swirling in his blue eyes and snatched her towel back, covering herself. "Oh, no, you don't. We shouldn't."

"Oh, but we should."

"We *can't.*"

"Not the way I'd like, but we most certainly can." Joshua reached for her. "Derrick invited himself. If he has to wait on the doorstep, I say let him wait. He's lucky to have a free place to stay."

"You've got a point. Let him wait," Victoria echoed, and dropped the towel.

Her ten minutes stretched to twenty, but that included the diversion engineered by Joshua. Never in a million years had she imagined she'd respond to a man the way she responded to him—with complete abandon. God, what would her mother have said about her behavior? A guest had been expected at any moment, but she'd made love to Joshua rather than get ready to answer the door. Victoria smiled. And she'd do it again in a heartbeat.

While she was applying makeup, she heard Derrick Tremont arrive. Not that she'd intended to eavesdrop, but the commotion was hard to miss since

Joshua had left the bedroom door cracked, and the agent had a big, booming voice. Especially when Joshua had explained that she'd be joining them for dinner.

"Lord, Joshua! I thought you'd sworn off women."

"I thought I had too, and then I met Victoria. . . ."

Unfortunately, she hadn't been able to hear any more because the conversation drifted out of the hallway and into the living room. With one last dab of perfume behind her ears, she rearranged the cowl neck on her soft red sweater and ran a hand lightly over the silver dolphin pin which was her only decoration.

Ready at last, she went out to meet the man that Joshua trusted enough to manage his publishing interests. Her smile was in place; clever chitchat was on the tip of her tongue. She walked on the balls of her feet so she didn't clump loudly across the hardwood floors. In short, she felt ready to make a bang-up first impression. Until she turned the corner of the living room and saw a strange man eagerly scanning her journal, guffawing at a section he must have thought particularly funny.

That's when her smile slipped. That's when the chitchat died a sudden death. That's when her next step reverberated through the house with a thud.

The middle-aged blond man looked up at the sudden noise and rose to his feet when he saw her. He gave her a big smile and said, "Well, hello. I'm Derrick Tremont. You must be Victoria, and this must be your journal." He waved her book back and forth in the air like a trophy.

"Hello, and yes, I'm Victoria Bennett. Where . . . where did you get my journal?"

Showing surprise at her tone, Derrick quickly explained. "Off the table. Joshua's outside, fiddling with the grill. He said to cool my jets and find something to read for a few minutes."

"You found it on the table?" Victoria echoed, and then guessed that Joshua had probably taken it out of her purse when he tried to find the earrings.

"Yes."

"That was a mistake," she explained as graciously as she could, and moved into the room with her hand outstretched for the diary.

"Mistake? I don't think so."

He was handing her back the book, when Joshua came back into the room. "What mistake?"

"My journal was on the table. Mr. Tremont—"

"Call me Derrick, please."

"Derrick found it and didn't realize it was a private journal." Sheer force of habit made Victoria smooth over the awkward situation.

"Oh, I realized it was private all right," Derrick told her bluntly and without any discernible remorse. "But it was also damn good. I thought Joshua left it out for me to discover."

"It was just a mistake," Victoria repeated.

"Mistake or not, I think we should do some talking."

Joshua moved stiffly toward the bar in the far corner. He needed a drink to settle the apprehension in his gut. He'd been betrayed too many times not to recognize the signs of a well-managed "mistake." The suspicious side of his nature was already halfway convinced that Victoria had staged the earring hunt, hoping to create exactly this situation. If that hadn't worked, she probably would have had Plan B waiting in the wings. He hadn't forgotten that she grew up in an atmosphere that rewarded fame.

"Can I get anyone else a drink?" Joshua asked as he passed them.

"Scotch if you've got it," Derrick told him, then looked at Victoria as if waiting for her to ask for something.

"Nothing for me."

"Then sit down, Victoria, and tell me how Joshua managed to find someone like you in the hills of Tennessee. You're gorgeous, smart, and you can write."

"I found Joshua, not the other way round. I was new, and he helped me learn the area." She directed a quick smile at Joshua. "I'm a certified nurse-midwife, not an aspiring writer. These pages are just my thoughts about my experiences since opening my practice."

Silently, Joshua saluted her for managing exactly the right amount of naïveté and genuine disbelief. With every passing second he was less certain of his trust in Victoria. Even after weeks of intimacy he still didn't *know* her, still couldn't read her emotions unless she wanted him to. The fact that he loved her made his nagging distrust all the more bitter to accept.

"Oh, but you are most definitely a writer," Derrick assured her, commanding Victoria's attention again. "Writing talent is the one thing I know."

Here it comes, thought Joshua as he approached with the drinks. *The surprised "Do you really think so?"* He handed Derrick his drink and resigned himself to whatever happened next. He'd heard this same kind of conversation too many times to count. If it wasn't over publishing, it was about academic appointments, publicity opportunities, or how best to utilize his abilities for someone else's benefit.

"I think you must be mistaken in my case," Victoria told his agent. "I don't know how anyone could possibly judge talent from a few pages of chicken scratching."

"I looked at more than a few pages. Besides, you've got something else going for you."

"What's that?" Victoria asked with a laugh.

"Joshua Logan, the mystique of the mountains, people's perceptions of rural Appalachia as a place of moonshiners, faith healers, and snake handlers."

"But it's not like that," protested Victoria.

"Who cares! I leafed through a lot of that journal, and I'm telling you, we can create a lightning strike with it. Knowing that you have a relationship with Joshua Logan will make this little story fly off the shelves! The bit with the healing touch in your kitchen was great."

Joshua's eyes narrowed as he realized how completely he had revealed himself to Victoria. And so had his grandmother. They'd said and shown her things that were never meant to be commercialized. He didn't blame his agent for trying to capitalize on opportunity; he blamed himself for creating the opportunity. This was a left hook that he'd walked right into.

"Joshua Logan is news," Derrick continued. "Especially after he finishes the publicity tour."

"I'm not doing the tour," Joshua said softly. "Not even the mini-tour. I told you that before you wasted your time coming here."

Derrick laughed and waved aside his comment. "A vacation is never a waste. What do you say, Victoria?"

She didn't say anything for a long time, then she started to chuckle. Finally, she laughed out loud and tried to frown at Joshua. "Okay, I deserve this for keeping you waiting. I'll admit, you guys had me going for a while. But I'm on to you now, so you can stop the kidding around."

At her laughter, the coldness in the pit of Joshua's stomach unexpectedly began to fade. It wasn't completely gone, but it no longer had a death grip on him.

"I'm not kidding, Victoria." Derrick kept pressing. "There really is a market for this kind of book if it's handled properly. Think about all the money that English fellow made with his little country-vet anecdotes! And I don't even think he had a psychic in his books!"

"Probably not, but he had something I don't have," Victoria told him patiently, her hands primly folded in her lap. "The desire to be published. This journal is for me. Period. I thank you for your kind words, and the opportunity, but *really* I don't think I'm interested."

Those words evaporated the lingering doubts, and Joshua smiled for the first time since coming into the room. Victoria was truly unique, a human being who didn't want her fifteen minutes of fame. He couldn't believe he'd finally found someone who preferred Joshua Logan to the connections that belonged to Indiana Jones.

He swirled the tobacco-colored liquid in his glass and observed, "The lady refused, Derrick. You'll have to take no for an answer twice tonight."

Derrick tossed back the last of his scotch and laughed. "I have not given up on you. I don't plan to take no for an answer until I believe you really understand how much damage you might do to your career if you refuse."

"Can you at least give up until after dinner?" Victoria cajoled. "If we make him mad, he's liable to burn our steaks."

She got a smile out of Derrick, who said, "In that case, consider the subject forgotten. But that means you'll have to come up with another topic of conversation."

"Like what?"

"Like what happened to all the tiny churches with snake pits? I didn't see a one on the way up here."

Victoria rolled her eyes. "You city people will believe anything, won't you?"

Quietly, Joshua smiled into his drink. Victoria was becoming one of "us" instead of one of "them."

❖————————❖

After dinner and a glass of wine, the three of them passed the time congenially enough. Joshua seemed unusually at ease with his agent, despite Derrick's occasional reference to publicity. They were like adversaries who had long ago worked out a code of ethics and admired each other almost to friendship.

All the same, Victoria was glad when a phone call from the hospital gave her an excuse to leave gracefully. Derrick was staying in Joshua's guest bedroom, and she wasn't quite sure how she felt about saying good night to the agent and toddling off to bed with Joshua. She'd spent a lot of nights in his bed, but somehow this was different.

Joshua had made it quite clear that his house was to be considered her home as much as the cabin, but that evening she'd felt a tension in Joshua that hadn't been there the day before. She attributed it to his need to get away from the world that was chasing him and trying to pull him back out there, where he had to live with echoes.

"Well, gentlemen, it's been a pleasure, but duty calls." She held her hand out to Derrick, who clasped it warmly. "It was nice meeting you."

"Don't tell me I won't see you again before I leave on Monday!"

"That depends entirely on the two pregnant women who are due to deliver in the next week." Without thought, she fished her keys out of her sweater. "They may preempt my time this weekend."

"You wear your keys?" Derrick asked.

"Just my truck key," Victoria told him with a grin.

"What's that other key?"

"Oh! I forgot. House key." She deliberately left out whose house the key unlocked. "I wear a house key and my truck key. Saves time when I need to get to the hospital, like now."

"Then I'll say good night and hope everything goes well."

"Good night."

"I'll walk you to the door," Joshua said, and put an arm around her. When they reached the threshold, he lifted her coat off the hook and stepped out on the porch with her. "How long will you be?"

Surprised, Victoria considered his question. Joshua, being fully aware that babies loved to wreak havoc with schedules, never asked questions like that. "I don't know. It's a second baby. Might only be three or four hours. Then again . . ."

"You might be all night," he finished for her.

"I might." It was an apology.

"How soon do you have to be there?"

Now Victoria knew something was wrong. "I don't have to leave this second, but I've got to go in the next few minutes."

"Damn. That doesn't give me much time." He shook his head as if disturbed by the idea and resigned to reality. But he didn't say anything else as he took her purse out of her hand to help her into her jacket and then handed it back to her.

Giving him an uncertain look, she slung the purse

over her shoulder and adjusted the strap. "Time for what?"

Joshua smiled at her and reached out with one of those strong hands to cup her jawline, letting it slide against his palm. The gesture was seductively innocent, more of a promise than a demand. She thought he was going to kiss her, but he didn't. He turned her world upside down instead.

"Victoria Elizabeth Radcliff Bennett, I love you. God knows I never thought to find you, but there you were right smack in the middle of my bed. And much too real to ignore." He lowered his voice to almost a reverent whisper. "There. I've said it out loud. I can't take it back even if I wanted to. I love you."

Victoria blinked and struggled to register the words. It had sounded like he'd said he loved her. Her heart sped up and slowed down before it settled into a rhythm of skipping beats. Finally, searching his eyes, she whispered, "Say that last part again."

Dropping his hand, he said in earnest, pronouncing each word distinctly so there could be no mistake. "I love you."

Silence grew between them, and Joshua watched her for some sign of emotion, some indication of how she really felt about his declaration. For Joshua, those three terrifying words had stripped him bare. There was no more pretending he could walk away. At least not whole. He'd given her his heart and now he had to wait because he couldn't feel Victoria's emotions.

Instead of the gentle, amazed kiss he was expecting, she thumped him on the chest. "And you pick *now* to tell me? With him in there and me having to go to the hospital!"

Joshua rubbed his chest and laughed at himself for expecting a normal reaction from a one-of-a-kind woman. "Would you rather I waited God knows how long until you came back?"

Instantly, Victoria looked stricken and said, "No."

"Now comes the hard part," Joshua said softly, and he brushed her hair back over her shoulder. "Do you love me?"

Victoria finally did kiss him on the lips and murmured, "Just my luck. I fall in love with a psychic who can't even tell that I've been head over heels in love with him for weeks."

"Joshua said I'd find you here to say good-bye," Derrick Tremont said as he walked into her Bodewell clinic early Monday morning and looked around curiously. "So this is what a midwife's practice looks like."

She got up from her table in the corner and joined him in the now-empty waiting room section of the big space. With a sweep of her arm around the room, she said, "Every modern convenience that I could beg, borrow, or steal."

"Looks like you're pretty good at begging, borrowing, and stealing."

"Fair to medium, I'd say. I had to be. Starting a practice is a pretty expensive proposition."

"Looks like you're doing okay," he said, and unbuttoned his camel's-hair overcoat.

"The people here have taken fairly well to me." Victoria crossed her arms. "Of course, to give credit where credit is due, Joshua helped."

"Oh, I think it took more than a little help from Joshua to win over the community." He gave her a direct gaze. "You're one of the most gracious women I've met in quite a while."

She returned his gaze just as directly, but with a crooked grin. "I could get used to your outrageous flattery, so don't spoil me."

"I'm telling you the plain, unembellished truth. Any other woman of my acquaintance would have screamed bloody murder to have found me ransacking her diary, but you tried to make excuses for me."

"I'm not much on screaming," Victoria admitted, and stooped to pick up a stray picture book, which she dropped into a plastic crate.

"I was serious about shopping that journal around as a proposal. If you'll put it in manuscript form, I'll represent you. We'll get some bites."

Victoria shook her head. "No. As I said, it's private."

"Then you should think about writing something not so private." Derrick pulled a card out of his pocket. "You have a gift for capturing people and moments. You're very real, Victoria, and you have a unique perspective, from what I've read. I mean that as a compliment."

She took his card but said, "You keep forgetting that I have a career that takes all my time and then some."

"You're as stubborn as Joshua, you know?"

"I take it you didn't get him to change his mind this morning?"

"The only thing I got out of this trip was a weekend vacation and his promise to consider a novel. He wouldn't budge on the publicity though." Derrick put his hands in his pants pockets and looked disapprovingly at her. "Like you and that damn journal."

He didn't intimidate her in the least because she'd gotten to know him better over the weekend. Derrick might be tall, pushy, and boisterous, but he was essentially a kind man. Only his concern for Joshua had dragged him out of New York to make sure his client understood the consequences of refusing the tour.

Except for dinner each day, she'd left them alone on Saturday and Sunday, so they could discuss business or anything else they wanted without an audience. She found that she'd needed the time alone to absorb the reality of falling in love with a man who loved her back. Joshua's declaration had turned her world upside down, but she hugged the words to her like a patch of sunshine on a winter day. This time she was going to get her happily-ever-after. Just like Joshua, she'd come home to the hills of Tennessee.

Realizing that Derrick was looking at her expectantly, she smiled. She'd enjoyed her time with him; he could be quite funny if somewhat single-minded about her journal. "I'll keep your card, but even if I were going to write a book, it wouldn't be fiction. It'd be something like a low-budget how-to manual for rural midwives. Something *I* could have used when I set up shop."

Derrick looked pensive for a moment and then said, "I don't have many contacts with university presses, which would probably be the place to start, but I'll make a few calls and put you in touch with someone who does deal with that kind of book."

"Oh, no! I wasn't . . . I couldn't ask you to do that."

"Why not? It's a couple of phone calls. Nothing more."

Flustered at being taken seriously, Victoria said, "The manual was just a thought."

Derrick winked at her. "So was the journal. I'm hoping you believe that one good turn deserves another. I'll let you know what I find out."

And then he was gone, leaving Victoria with the beginnings of an idea that wouldn't go away. How hard could it be to organize her thoughts, list her problems and how she solved them? She'd spent weeks sorting out good ideas from the bad already.

A tiny part of her even admitted that she might be considering this book so she could hold herself up as successful and anoint herself with glory to prove a point to her parents. Thoughtfully, Victoria dragged her attention back to her appointment schedule, warning herself not to start counting on a book that wasn't even definite.

For Joshua, having her near him was like having a charm that kept the echoes at bay, but the price he had to pay for his peace seemed too high. He'd lived his whole life knowing how other people felt, and now he could only sit and speculate as to why the woman he loved seemed edgy. He felt cheated somehow. Even though he pushed his mind to find her emotional echo, he came up empty. She'd learned to guard herself too well; he was still paying for another man's sins.

Victoria wandered aimlessly around the cabin, first turning on, then turning off lights. Something was bothering her. Something she couldn't or wouldn't talk about. He wasn't certain if she was anxious, sad, worried, guilty, or any of the other hundred emotions that would account for her behavior. Joshua kept waiting for her to settle and talk to him, but even when she sat down, she didn't grow calm or conversational. Victoria worried the edge of the sofa arm, running her finger up and down the piping. She'd been distracted during dinner, and now she was almost withdrawn.

When the phone rang, she jumped, crossed quickly to the bed, and snatched it up, only to find out it was a wrong number. Slowly she replaced the receiver.

"Expecting a call?"

She shrugged. "I've got a couple of patients due anytime now. Like Granny says—trouble don't come single."

"Something else wrong?"

"Not really. Just tired, I guess. I've been thinking

too much today." She turned her mouth up at the corners in a forced smile.

"About what?" Joshua joined her on the bed and pulled her back into his arms as he braced himself against the headboard.

She snuggled into his embrace easily, as if she had always belonged there. "About life, the universe, glory, intuition, choices, and midwifery."

"Just the usual stuff, then," he teased, and let himself drink in the scent of her.

"Just the usual," she echoed. "All that stuff a person has to decide for herself."

As always, his body responded with enthusiasm to the nearness of Victoria. Even without perfume she was an incredible combination of fragrances from shampoo to soap, everything enhanced by some indefinable essence that was Victoria alone. All of his senses knew her. He carried her image in his mind. Her voice was unmistakable in its sexuality. His hands knew every bump, every curve of her body. He knew her taste just as he knew her scent—intimately. All of his senses knew her, except for one, except for the one sense that made him more and less than the rest of the world.

He loved her. He lay here with her in bed as she rested her head trustingly on his chest. She loved him. What more did he want?

Joshua knew what he wanted, and what he couldn't have—a piece of her soul, her secrets, for himself. A piece that no one else had ever had or ever would again. He wanted the openness that seemed to exist only at the moment of climax. He wanted Victoria to give freely what she gave by instinct when he made love to her.

He couldn't walk away, so he'd have to learn how to deal with the silence of her echo. Somehow. He rested his chin on the top of her head. She barely stirred. The long hours lately were taking their toll, and he wondered if this practice was really everything she'd dreamed of having.

"How long has it been since you've seen a movie?"

"I think it was *Robin Hood*. The one with Errol Flynn."

He chuckled. "Good, then the ones at Bodewell's new triplex will seem like first-run movies to you. If we go before five tomorrow, we get the early bird discount and two-for-one popcorn." He felt her smile against his chest at his suggestion for a brief second.

"Nice idea, but Amanda Shipman's one of the patients due to deliver this week," she said sleepily, and shifted up to look at him in apology. "And I have a feeling that she'll go tomorrow. I wouldn't want you to get your heart set on an uninterrupted date."

"I have my heart set on only one thing."

"What's that?"

Joshua rolled her beneath him and showed her.

All day Victoria waited for the service to call her at the Mention clinic and tell her that Amanda was in labor. All day the twinge of concern she had for Amanda grew, and yet she couldn't pin it down to anything specific. Everything should be fine. Even if Amanda went into another postpartum hemorrhage, she was ready. She knew what to do. Everything necessary would be prepped and available long before it was ever needed.

Then why couldn't she shake this feeling that Amanda's delivery was going to end badly?

She checked her watch and knew she had to get on the road to Bodewell if she was going to meet Joshua at her office for the early movie. As she walked in the door and dropped her files on the table, she expected the phone to ring. It didn't. The call didn't come until they were standing in the popcorn line. A young girl wearing a white shirt, blue skirt, and theater name tag hovered nervously at the edge of the small crowd waiting for the movie and said, "Victoria Bennett? I have a call for Victoria Bennett."

She raised her hand and said to Joshua, "Let me know how this one ends. I have a feeling that I'm out of here."

"This lady called." The young girl held out a scrap of paper as she came over. "She said for you to call her real quick."

"Thanks." One brief phone call to the answering service was followed by a longer one to the hospital. "Kathy? Hi. This is Victoria. You guys are about to get one of my patients, Amanda Shipman. The service said she was already on her way. This is baby number four."

Victoria shook her head. "Trust me. You don't want to catch this baby before I get there. Amanda's a grandmulti with a history of postpartum hemorrhage. That is not a good combination. I want you to alert Wally Grenwald to be prepared for a *stat* call. Yeah, draw a type and crossmatch just in case we need blood." Victoria smiled. "You're a jewel, Kathy."

When she hung up, Joshua said, "Let's roll. Sounds like a busy night. I'll drop you at the hospital. It'll save time. You can call me when you're done, and we'll collect your car then."

Victoria gave him a grateful smile. She never had to explain her priorities to Joshua. He just always seemed to know.

Joshua dropped his keys on his desk and resigned himself to an evening without Victoria. He jabbed the blinking message button on the answering machine and leaned back in the chair at his desk. The first message was from the service trying to track down Victoria. The second was from his grandmother—no message. The third caller was Derrick. His message brought Joshua straight up in his chair.

"Hi, Joshua. This is Derrick. When I gave Victoria my card, I forgot to get hers. So give her a message for me. I've got a couple of people interested in this puppy. She should call me as soon as possible to discuss details before she loses her nerve."

ELEVEN

Before she loses her nerve. Her nerve to do what? The question answered itself—publish that damned journal.

"No." Joshua's denial was firm, spoken aloud to give it more weight, but it was a small word and the doubt that had crept into his heart was big.

Reaching for the machine, he replayed the message, focusing his whole attention on finding another meaning for Derrick's breezy instructions beyond the obvious one. He didn't bother to listen to it a third time. Slowly he got out of the chair and walked a small circle, trying to control his suspicions and failing miserably. The past caved in on him, echoing a bitter chorus of I-told-you-sos.

No matter how hard he tried to conjure another explanation, there was only one conclusion to be drawn from the tape. Victoria had betrayed him. *Last night she'd paced the floor and jumped for the phone.* He felt his fingers curl with the need to push back time and keep himself safe from this moment. But that was impossible. He'd said yes when he should have said no. He'd let a sultry voice and clear gray eyes make him forget that human nature was impossible to fight.

Angry at his weakness, he snatched the keys off the desk. He'd be damned if he'd wait by the phone for her to call. When he strode outside, he slammed the door, but it didn't take the bitterness away. He could still taste it as he threw a leg over the motorcycle and turned the key, feeling it roar to life beneath him, dangerous and angry.

That's how he felt—dangerous and angry. Maybe if he drove fast enough, he wouldn't be able to feel at all. That's what he hoped, but his mind wouldn't let go of the facts. Wouldn't stop thinking.

She was willing to take what was private between them and sell it to the highest bidder. All her talk of not needing money or fame had been a smoke screen. She never let down her guard with him—not because of Richard—but because she'd been afraid of what he'd see. Deep inside where it counted, she was just like everyone else, with her share of manipulation and greed. Hungry to become the perfect daughter again and impress her parents. Or maybe it was simply that Derrick had worn her down.

Not that it mattered. Regardless of why or how she'd decided to sensationalize her connection to him, she'd done it knowing that he wanted to maintain some semblance of privacy. She'd done it knowing that her actions would destroy the fragile trust he had in her. She'd done it knowing that her journal might expose his grandmother to ridicule. And she hadn't cared.

Halfway to the hospital he realized that what he resented the most was the fact that she'd taken away his dream of growing old with the woman he loved by his side. A woman with that kind of ambition wasn't going to stay on the mountain, and even if she stayed, he wasn't sure he'd ever be able to trust her again.

He passed a moth-eaten road sign and vividly remembered what it felt like to be young and angry and drunk and stupid.

At the hospital, he left word with the nurses that he was in the waiting room, so they could relay the message to Victoria when she came out of delivery. Anyone looking into the small room would have mistaken him for an expectant father. By turns he paced stoically or sat in one of the two chairs. He stayed away from the sofa because the springs were obviously shot.

Not that it mattered where he sat or how much he paced. No one else was in the room. Amanda Shipman's husband was probably coaching his wife. But that was all right. Joshua was in the mood to be alone.

When Victoria finally came in, he'd been contemplating the toes of his boots for twenty minutes and trying to decide how to say what he wanted to say.

"You didn't have to come up and wait here," she said as she reached up and pulled off the surgical cap.

She looked tired but happy, as if she'd gotten unexpected good news. Her hair was caught in a braid at the back, and she still wore blue scrubs. Then she gave him the innocent smile that had fooled him from day one and said, "But I'm glad you did."

By inches, Joshua eased himself out of the chair, cautioning himself to hold on to his temper, to wait. He didn't walk toward her, but he asked, "How's the patient?"

"She had some hemorrhaging, but we shut it down fairly quickly."

He nodded. "Good."

Victoria felt an awful silence expand inside the room, and suddenly she realized that the apprehension she'd been experiencing for the past two days was back. And this time it had nothing to do with Amanda. She took a step toward him with her hand outstretched. "Is . . . is something wrong?"

"You could say that." Joshua's voice was steady; his gaze never strayed from hers. "Derrick called. He left a brief message for you."

Inexplicably, a cold knot settled in her stomach as she said, "He did?"

"He said he's drummed up interest in your book, and you should call him before you lose your nerve."

A memory assailed her, and she dropped her hand slowly. She'd played this scene before, at the cabin the day she met him, when he stared at her and waited for an explanation. Only this time there wasn't even a hint of amusement in Joshua's blue eyes. They were icy cold and judgmental. He expected—*no, believed*—the worst of her. He listened to a cryptic message and believed she used his contacts to sell a gimmicky commercial book that exploited him.

Joshua's unspoken accusation sunk painful claws in her heart that tore at her each time she took a breath. How could he believe for even a second that she would use him like that? She lifted her chin and tilted her head back slightly to discourage tears. If she'd been another woman, she might have tried to hurt him back. But she knew Joshua was already hurting.

He didn't trust her any more today than he had when he'd found her on his bed. His willingness to believe in her betrayal forced Victoria to face a hard reality. No matter how much she loved him, she couldn't make him trust her. And until he trusted his heart and her love, they had no future.

By nature, we're a suspicious lot, he'd told her when describing his roots. She knew only too well that people didn't change just because you wanted them to change. How many years had she wasted telling herself that Richard would change, that she could make him understand if she tried a little harder? Too many, and never again.

This time she wanted it all or nothing. She wanted something built on faith, rock solid, and damned near indestructible. Because of that, she decided not to explain about the midwifery manual. If she did, she'd be explaining every word, every action for the rest of her life. Instead, as calmly as she could, she asked, "Is that all he said?"

Joshua's response was scathing. "What more do

you need to hear? You got what you wanted. You used me to get it, but I don't guess that matters to you."

It mattered more than he could possibly guess, but she could not, *would not* tell him. He had to find his way through the maze of doubt all alone. It was the only way she could ever be sure that he wouldn't always be questioning her love. Standing there, silently absorbing the scorn in his expression, took every ounce of willpower she had.

When she didn't defend herself, Joshua chided her. "Surely you have a explanation?"

"No, I don't need one. You seem to have everything all figured out. You heard the message."

"Then it is true." Until that moment Joshua hadn't realized how much he was counting on Victoria's denial, how much he had wanted reasonable explanations or righteous indignation. Anything but the calm with which she faced him. "I trusted you, Victoria."

"No, you didn't." One tear threatened to escape her control, but she covered it by rubbing her face as if she were weary of covering the same ground again and again. "That's what it all comes down to between us, Joshua."

"Then tell me I'm wrong. Tell me why!"

"My answer's not going to change anything." Both of them stood there, locked in place by their need for absolutes. From that moment there was no going back.

"I guess that's all the answer I need," Joshua said bitterly as he walked by her and out the door.

"It's the answer you deserve," she said quietly when the door clicked loudly into place.

Every cell in her body screamed at her to go after him and explain before it was too late. But she couldn't go running after him. If she did, their relationship would never have that granite foundation. No, Joshua would have to find his way back himself. The one thing she knew with complete certainty was that if Joshua came back, it had to be because his belief in her love was stronger than his fear of betrayal.

As the tears finally fell, Victoria whispered, "For once in your life, Joshua, believe in something you can't touch."

Despite the late hour, Lara Logan was dressed and waiting for her grandson before he even knocked on her door. She'd known he was coming; she knew her grandson better than anybody on earth knew him, except maybe Victoria. But she didn't hold out much hope on that front, not after the black dreams she'd had that night. The chance was slipping away; her heart was squeezing her too hard lately. She was tired of hoping; it was time to go home. It was time to say good-bye.

When J.J. knocked, she pulled herself up out of the rocker and went to the door. They never wasted many words between them. Talk didn't seemed particularly useful. Lara didn't bother to ask him in or to sit down. He'd do those things in his own good time just as he would tell her what brought him out in the dead of night. J.J. was in a mood to pace, so she got out of his way, settled herself on the couch, and waited until he'd worked himself up to the sticking point.

Surprising her, he paced only a moment before he told her, "Victoria used her relationship with me to finagle a book deal about her experiences as a midwife."

"Clever girl."

"Very smart, our Victoria," Joshua agreed. "The gimmick she used is her unique personal insight into me and maybe you as her medicine woman sidekick." He sighed heavily with regret. The sound was laced with pain. "I've made a mistake, Gran."

"I imagine you have," Lara told him softly, knowing full well what his mistake was even if he didn't. "Can you make it right?"

He laughed, intimating that the task was impossible. "I don't think so. I can't call back time."

"And if you could?"

For a moment he stopped pacing and faced her. "I wouldn't have trusted Victoria Bennett. I wouldn't fall in love with her."

"And what would that change? You'd still be alone."

"I'd be whole," he answered, and picked up a photo from the credenza, running his thumb along the frame before putting it down. "God knows, I'm tired of losing pieces of myself."

"Then maybe it's time you stopped holding back and gave everything you are to someone who will cherish the gift."

That advice brought Joshua up short. He would have argued with her, except for the feelings that swamped him as he rested a hand against the back of her empty rocker. His talent flared to life, and in the split second before he pulled his hand away, an overwhelming impression of a dying woman invaded his consciousness. An impression of a woman whose will to live was the only thing that kept her strong, and now her will was slipping away, fading into nothing.

The sensation was so powerful, he closed his eyes against the wave of emotion that hit him. Sorrow sliced through his soul, leaving a chill in its wake. When he had control of himself again, he put the image together with the knowledge that the rocker belonged to his grandmother. Gran lifted one eyebrow slightly when he opened his eyes and focused on her. The sense of loss he experienced was profound, and his mind refused to accept what his touch had revealed.

"Why?" he asked.

"There it is again. You deny your talent, but you never have been able to make it go away. Have you, J.J.?"

He ignored the question as he put both hands on the back of the rocker, knowing what he'd feel, but he didn't pull away this time. He had to know that he hadn't misread the touch. Finally, he snatched his hands back. His grandmother was dying, and she wasn't doing a damn thing to hold on. This time he almost shouted the word. *"Why?"*

"No one lives forever." She was almost matter-of-fact about her answer, as if he had asked what time it was.

"But why now?" Joshua couldn't even begin to imagine a world without her sly smile and sharp mind. "Why give up?"

"Because I've run out of time, J.J. I've spent twenty years waiting for you to make peace with yourself. We have a gift, you and I. A gift that came from my mother, who got it from her father. It's a gift you never wanted, and I'm sorry for that."

Lara paused a moment before adding, "The mountain taught us that one season feeds the next. What came before has meaning because of what comes after. I would like to have seen the talent pass on. Victoria's a fine woman. I'm sorry for that too."

Stunned, Joshua began to pace again, trying to make some sense of what she told him. "You're ready to let your life slip away because I've ended my relationship with a woman? Which means you can't pass on this curse of ours?"

"No, that's too simple. What I'm telling you . . . well, it's not blackmail," Lara told him softly, and held out her hand for her grandson to join her on the sofa. When he did and she held both his big hands in her frail, arthritic ones, she said as gently as she could, "I'm old. I'm tired. I can't wait forever. I thought you of all people would understand how the past creates the future. I want to do more than see the future, Joshua John. I want to touch my future, your children. But you're so worried about the present, you refuse the future."

"That's not—"

"Hush. For once I have the tell of this, and you're going to listen. You can't shut out the world just because it isn't perfect. You always hated knowing people's flaws. You didn't want to see them. Maybe that's why you've lived in the past all these years with your artifacts and your bits of broken pottery. Because you can know their secrets and never have to face those people, or forgive them, or accept them."

She let go of his hands and folded hers in her lap. "You think about that when you're alone. The rest of your life is a long time to be alone, Joshua John."

For the first time, Joshua considered his psychic abilities for what they were—a thread from the past, part of a legacy that had been woven before he was born and bound him to the future. He rested his shoulders against the couch and let his head fall back. He was trying to run away from his heritage. That's what Gran thought, and maybe she was right.

"If you hold on to fear," Lara warned him, "you can't hold on to what you love with both hands. And, believe me, it takes both hands to hold on to forever."

Closing his eyes, Joshua said, "That's a lot to ask. If I let go of caution, I could fall."

"Or you could catch the future."

The possibility hung in the air between them. As Joshua accepted that she was right, he knew he had to reach out. He had to make *one* connection, *one* bond that could never be broken. He had to believe in someone. Love someone unconditionally. Trust someone. Like Victoria had. The enormity of what he'd said to her closed in on him and he shook his head. "I've made a mistake, Gran."

"I imagine you have, but can you put it right?"

"I don't know, Gran. I don't know."

Joshua slowed the motorcycle and looked down into the hollow. Light shone through the cabin windows, and Victoria's truck was parked in front. Midnight had come and gone, but she was still awake. Abruptly, he turned the bike onto the driveway. Waiting until tomorrow would only give the hurt more time to fester. If he had any chance of proving to Victoria that his love was unconditional, he had to do it now, before any more time passed.

When he killed the engine, the door opened and Victoria was silhouetted in the opening. He waited for her to tell him to leave, but she didn't. She stood quietly, wrapped in an afghan instead of a robe and wearing that mantle of calm he remembered from their first meeting. The opening move was his, and he didn't think he'd get a second chance.

He climbed off the bike and approached the porch, stopping at the base of the steps. A dozen apologies came to mind, and none were worth the breath it would take to say them. None of them said what needed to be said. So, when he looked at her, he said what was in his heart instead and trusted her to understand him.

"Blind faith is what you're asking of me, Vicky. Blind faith. And it scares the hell out of me."

Victoria closed her eyes briefly and drew the first steady breath she'd taken in hours. The vise around her heart eased its grip as Joshua put his foot on the first stair and climbed one step closer. Silently, she willed him on and warned herself that he hadn't come all the way. Yet.

"I've spent my life knowing what was in other people's hearts. But not yours." Joshua stabbed his fingers through his hair. Emotion was raw in his voice. "I fell in love with you, but I don't know what's in your heart, Victoria. I can't see inside; I can't touch your feelings. So what you're asking of me, I've never had to give. I'm never going to stop wanting to touch the part of you that is hidden from me, but I can accept the fact I may never be able to."

He climbed another step, and Victoria fell in love with him all over again because he didn't ask her to open her emotions and prove herself to him. He wasn't trying to test her. She could see the tension that tightened his muscles as he came closer to the point of no return, but he didn't falter. The inner strength she knew was there held him up and pushed him forward.

"Vicky, until half an hour ago I didn't think I could trust someone without reservation, but I found out something tonight. Gran helped me see this part. The only thing that scares me more than blindly trusting anyone is the thought of losing you and our future." As he stepped up onto the porch, he said, "I don't care if you write a million books about me, because none of them could ever hurt me. Not if you wrote them. I know you'd never hurt me. It may be a little late to say I trust you, but I do."

"It's not too late," she told him. Victoria could scarcely breathe by the time he stopped a few inches from her. She could see the truth of everything he'd said written on his face. He meant every word. When she started to speak again, he laid a finger against her lips.

"No explanations. I don't want to know. Not tonight anyway." He moved his finger away from her lips and down her neck. His blue eyes were dark and full of need. "All I want to do is hold you. Know that you're real. Know that I haven't lost you."

Without a word Victoria dropped the afghan as she went into his arms, letting the warmth of his body chase away the chill that had shivered up her spine when he confessed he needed her. She finally let go of the ache that had replaced her heartbeat since he walked away from her in the hospital and dropped the last of her defenses. "I'm real, and I'm right where you left me."

"I'm glad," Joshua whispered into her hair as unfamiliar emotions flooded through him—Victoria's emotions. The torrent was a jumble of love and hope and faith. It was the one connection he'd been looking for his entire life. All the dark places inside him were gone, blown away by Victoria's love and belief in him. He was almost shaking at the thought of coming so close to losing her forever. Finally the feelings settled into a warmth that suffused his soul and made him whole.

"I'm glad you're right where I left you," he repeated almost fiercely. "Because I'm not letting go again. I want all of it, Victoria. Marriage and kids and puppies."

Victoria's heart jumped into her throat, but she didn't lift her head. She tried to make her tone light as she said, "You can't be serious. All those echoes bouncing off your walls? All that clutter messing up your pretty house?"

"I don't give a damn if you trash the place as long as you say yes," he said in a voice that warned her he was serious.

Looking up, she searched his face, trying to convince herself that she was actually going to get everything she wanted. "Have you forgotten what I said about midwifery being the acid test of a relationship?"

"Love, we've just passed the acid test of our relationship. So . . ." he murmured as he brushed his lips against hers. "Will you marry me or not?" He tilted her head up and kissed her, finding his answer in the sweetness of her kiss and the movement of her body against his. He let go of the past and held on to forever with both hands.

TWELVE

Settled in her rocking chair, Lara Logan waited on her porch, noticing that the mist was strong for a late summer morning. Beyond that brief observation, she paid no attention to the tendrils of vapor that clung to the hollows of the mountain, playing a peculiar game of hide-and-seek with the sun. Instead, her attention was focused on a sight she never thought she'd live to see.

Her great-granddaughter.

J.J. carried her naturally, without apprehension, and Victoria walked beside him. The look of contentment on his face was nothing compared to the contentment Lara could feel in his soul as he approached her rocking chair. When he put the baby in her arms, Lara soothed the child's cry at being disturbed. Tiny fingers grazed her cheek, and from the first touch Lara knew. She smiled. The wheel of life had turned again.

Slowly she began to rock the baby, humming a song that had no name. After the baby's eyes closed, she exchanged a look with Victoria and nodded. They understood each other, always had. They both had the same goals.

"We've finally decided on a name," Victoria told her as she took her husband's hand. "Lara Elizabeth Logan."

Lara swallowed past the lump in her throat as she looked down at her namesake, whose mouth opened and closed on an imaginary meal. Heaven would have to wait a while yet. This little one needed her more.

THE EDITOR'S CORNER

What an irresistible lineup we have for you next month! These terrific romances from four of our most talented authors deliver wonderful heroines and sexy heroes. They are full of passion, fun, and intensity—just what you need to keep warm on those crisp autumn nights.

Starting things off is **ONE ENCHANTED AUTUMN**, LOVESWEPT #710, from supertalented Fayrene Preston, and enchanted is exactly how Matthew Stone feels when he meets the elegant attorney Samantha Elliott. She's the one responsible for introducing his aunt to her new beau, and wary that the beau might be a fortune hunter, Matthew is determined to stop the wedding. Samantha invites Matthew to dinner, sure that seeing the loving couple together will convince the cynical reporter, but she soon finds herself the object of Matthew's own amorous pursuit. Another utterly romantic novel of unexpected passion and exquisite sensuality from Fayrene.

Billie Green is back with **STARWALKER**, LOVESWEPT #711, a unique and sexy romance that'll have you spellbound. Born of two bloods, torn between two worlds, Marcus Aurelius Reed is arrogant, untamed—and the only man who can save Laken Murphy's brother's life. She needs a Comanche shaman to banish an unseen evil, but he refuses to help her, swears the man she seeks no longer exists. Her persistence finally pays off, but the real challenge begins when Laken agrees to share his journey into a savage past. Tempted by this lord of dark secrets, Laken must now trust him with her wild heart. Once more Billie seduces her fans with this enthralling story of true love.

Victoria Leigh gives us a heroine who only wants to be **BLACKTHORNE'S WOMAN**, LOVESWEPT #712. Micah Blackthorne always captures his quarry, but Bethany Corbett will do anything to elude her pursuer and keep her baby safe—risk her life on snowy roads, even draw a gun! But once she understands that he is her only chance for survival, she pleads for a truce and struggles to prove her innocence. Micah refuses to let his desire for the beautiful young mother interfere with his job, but his instincts tell him she is all she claims to be . . . and more. In a world of betrayal and dark desire, only he can command her surrender—and only she can possess his soul. Victoria has created a thrilling tale of heated emotions, racing pulses, and seductive passions that you won't be able to put down.

Please give a big welcome to Elaine Lakso, whose debut novel will have you in **HIGH SPIRITS**,

LOVESWEPT #713. Cody McRae is tall, dark, dangerously unpredictable—and the only man Cass MacFarland has ever loved! Now, six years after he's accused her of betrayal, she is back in town . . . and needs his help to discover if her spooky house is truly haunted. As wickedly handsome as ever, Cody bets Cass he is immune to her charms—but taking his dare might mean getting burned by the flames in his eyes. Funny, outrageous, and shamelessly sexy, this wonderful novel offers spicy suspense and two unforgettable characters whose every encounter strikes romantic sparks.

Happy reading!

With warmest wishes,

Beth de Guzman

Beth de Guzman

Senior Editor

P.S. Don't miss the women's novels coming your way in October. In the blockbuster tradition of Julie Garwood, **THIEF OF HEARTS** by Teresa Medeiros is a captivating historical romance of adventure and triumph; **VIRGIN BRIDE** by Tamara Leigh is an electrifying medieval romance in which a woman falls in love with her mortal enemy; **COURTING MISS HATTIE** by award-winning author Pamela Morsi is an unforgettable novel in which handsome Reed Tylor shares a scorching kiss with Hattie Colfax and realizes that his best friend is the only woman he will ever love. We'll be giving you a sneak peek at these wonderful books in next month's LOVESWEPTs. And immediately following this page, look for a preview of the terrific romances from Bantam that are *available now!*

Don't miss these phenomenal books by
your
favorite Bantam authors

On sale in August:

THE LAST BACHELOR
by Betina Krahn

PRINCE OF WOLVES
by Susan Krinard

WHISPERED LIES
by Christy Cohen

"One of the genre's most creative writers. Her ingenious romances always entertain and leave readers with a warm glow."
—*Romantic Times*

Betina Krahn

THE LAST BACHELOR

Betina Krahn, author of the national bestsellers THE PRINCESS AND THE BARBARIAN and MY WARRIOR'S HEART, is one of the premier names in romance. Now, with this spectacularly entertaining battle of the sexes, her distinctive humor and charm shine brighter than ever.

Antonia's bedroom was a masterpiece of Louis XIV opulence . . . in shades of teal and seafoam and ecru, with touches of gilt, burnt umber, and apricot. Sir Geoffrey had spared no expense to see to her pleasure and her comfort: from the hand-tinted friezes on the ceilings, to the ornate floor-to-ceiling bed, to the thick Aubusson carpets, to the exquisite tile stove, hand-painted with spring flowers, he had imported from Sweden to insure the room would be evenly warm all winter. Every shape, every texture was lush and feminine, meant to delight her eye and satisfy her touch . . . the way her youth and beauty and energy had delighted her aging husband. It was her personal retreat, a balm for her spirits, her sanctuary away from the world.

And Remington Carr had invaded it.

When she arrived breathless at her chamber door, she could see that the heavy brocades at the windows had been gathered back and the south-facing windows had been thrown open to catch the sultry breeze. Her hand-painted and gilded bed was mounded with bare ticking, and her linens, comforters, and counterpane were piled in heaps on the floor around the foot of the bed. It took a moment to locate Remington.

He stood by her dressing table with his back to her, his shirt sleeves rolled up and his vest, cravat, and collar missing. The sight of his long, black-clad legs and his wide, wedge-shaped back sent a distracting shiver through her. When his head bent and his shoulder flexed, she leaned to one side to see what he was doing.

He was holding one of her short black gloves and as she watched, he brought it to his nose, closed his eyes, and breathed in. A moment later, he strolled to the nearby bench, where her shot-silk petticoat and French-cut corset—the purple satin one, covered with black Cluny lace—lay exactly as she had left them the evening before. She looked on, horrified, as he lifted and wiggled the frilly hem of her petticoat, watching the delicate flounces wrap around his wrist. Abandoning that, he ran a speculative hand over the molded cups at the top of her most elegant stays, then dragged his fingers down the front of them to toy with the suspenders that held up her stockings. She could see his smile in profile.

"No garters," he murmured, just loud enough to hear in the quiet.

"Just what do you think you are doing?" she demanded, lurching forward a step before catching herself.

He turned sharply, then relaxed into a heart-stopping smile at the sight of her.

"Women's work . . . what else?" he said in insufferably pleasant tones. "I've just given your featherbeds a sound thrashing, and I am waiting for the dust to clear so I can get on with turning your mattresses."

"My mattresses don't need turning, thank you," she charged, her face reddening. "No more than my most personal belongings need plundering. How dare you invade my bedchamber and handle my things?" She was halfway across the room before she realized he wasn't retreating, and that, in fact, the gleam in his eyes intensified as she approached, making it seem that he had been waiting for her. Warnings sounded in her better sense and she halted in the middle of the thick carpet.

"Put those back"—she pointed to the gloves in his hand—"and leave at once."

He raised one eyebrow, then glanced at the dainty black seven-button glove he held. "Only the best Swedish kid, I see. One can always tell Swedish glove leather by the musk that blends so nicely with a woman's own scent. Your scent is roses, isn't it?" He inhaled the glove's scent again and gave her a desirous look. "I do love roses."

He was teasing, flirting with her again . . . the handsome wretch. It was no good appealing to his sense of shame; where women were concerned, he didn't seem to have one. Her only hope, she realized, was to maintain her distance and her composure and use deflating candor to put him in his place. And his place, she told her racing heart, was anywhere *except* the middle of her bedroom.

"You rush headlong from one outrage into another, don't you, your lordship?" she declared, crossing her arms and resisting the hum of excitement rising in her blood. "You haven't the slightest regard for decency or propriety—"

"I do wish you would call me Remington," he said with exaggerated sincerity. "I don't think a first-name-basis would be considered too much familiarity with a man who is about to climb into your bed and turn it upside down." Trailing that flagrant double entendre behind him, he tossed her glove aside and started for the bed.

"Into my . . . ?" Before she could protest, he was indeed climbing up into the middle of her bed, pushing the featherbed to the foot of the bed and seizing the corners of the mattress. As the ropes shifted and groaned and the thick mattress began to roll, she felt a weightless sensation in the pit of her stomach and understood that he was moving more than just a cotton-stuffed ticking. The sight of him in those vulnerable confines was turning her inside out, as well.

"Come down out of there this instant, Remington Carr!" She hurried to the edge of the bed, frantic to get him out of it.

"I have a better idea," he said, shoving to his feet and bracing his legs to remain stable on the springy ropes. "Why don't you come up here? There's plenty of room." He flicked a suggestive look around him, then pinned it on her. "You know, this is a very large bed for a woman who sleeps by herself. How long has it been, Antonia, since you've had your ticking turned?"

A romance of mystery, magic,
and forbidden passion

PRINCE OF WOLVES
by
Susan Krinard

"A brilliantly talented new author."
—*Romantic Times*

*Through with running from the past, Joelle Randall had
come to the rugged Canadian Rockies determined to face
her pain and begin anew. All she needed was a guide to
lead her through the untamed mountain wilderness to the
site where her parents' plane had crashed so long ago. But
the only guide Joelle could find was Luke Gévaudan, a
magnetically attractive loner with the feral grace of a wolf
and eyes that glittered with a savage intensity. She couldn't
know that Luke was the stuff of legends, one of the last
survivors of an ancient race of werewolves . . . a man
whose passion she would not be able to resist—no matter
how terrible the price.*

Joey was too lost in her own musings to immediately
notice the sudden hush that fell over the bar. The
absence of human chatter caught her attention slowly,
and she blinked as she looked around. The noisy
clumps of men were still at their tables, but they

seemed almost frozen in place. Only the television, nearly drowned out before, broke the quiet.

There was a man standing just inside the doorway, as still as all the others, a silhouette in the dim light. It took Joey a moment to realize that he was the focus of this strange and vivid tableau.

Even as the thought registered, someone coughed. It broke the hush like the snap of a twig in a silent forest. The room suddenly swelled again with noise, a relieved blast of sound as things returned to normal.

Joey turned to Maggie.

"What was that all about?" she asked. Maggie was slow to answer, but the moment of gravity was short-lived, and the barkeep smiled again and shook her head.

"Sorry about that. Must have seemed pretty strange, I guess. But he tends to have that effect on people around here."

Joey leaned forward on her elbow, avoiding a wet puddle on the counter. "Who's 'he'?" she demanded, casting a quick glance over her shoulder.

Setting down the mug she'd been polishing, Maggie assumed an indifference Joey was certain she didn't feel. "His name is Luke Gévaudan. He lives some way out of town—up the slope of the valley. Owns a pretty big tract of land to the east."

Joey slewed the stool around to better watch the man, chin cupped in her hand. "I know you've said people here don't much care for outsiders," she remarked, "but you have to admit that was a pretty extreme reaction. . . . Gévaudan, you said. Isn't that a French name?"

"French-Canadian," Maggie corrected.

"So he's one of these . . . French-Canadians? Is

that why the people here don't like him?" She studied Maggie over her shoulder.

"It's not like that," Maggie sighed. "It's hard to explain to someone from outside—I mean, he's strange. People don't trust him, that's all. And as a rule he doesn't make much of an attempt to change that. He keeps to himself."

Unexpectedly intrigued, Joey divided her attention between the object of her curiosity and the redhead. "Don't kid me, Maggie. He may be strange and he may be standoffish, but you can't tell me that wasn't more than just mild distrust a minute ago."

Maggie leaned against the bar and sagged there as if in defeat. "I said it's complicated. I didn't grow up here, so I don't know the whole story, but there are things about the guy that bother people. I hear he was a strange kid." She hesitated. "He's also got a bit of a reputation as a—well, a ladykiller, I guess you could say." She grinned and tossed her red curls. "I'm not sure that's the right word. Let's put it this way—he's been known to attract the ladies, and it's caused a bit of a ruckus now and then."

"Interesting," Joey mused. "If he's so popular with the local women, I can see why the men around here wouldn't be overly amused."

"It's not just local women," Maggie broke in, falling naturally into her usual habit of cozy gossip. "Though there were a couple of incidents—before my time, you understand. But I know there've been a few outsiders who've, shall we say, taken up with him." She gave an insinuating leer. "They all left, every one of them, after a few months. And none of them ever talked."

Wondering when she'd get a clear look at his face, Joey cocked an eye at her friend. "I guess that could make for some resentment. He may be mysterious, but he doesn't sound like a very nice guy to me."

"There you go," Maggie said, pushing herself off the bar. "Consider yourself warned." She winked suggestively. "The way you're staring at him, I'd say you need the warning."

At Joey's start of protest, Maggie sashayed away to serve her customers. Joey was left to muse on what she'd been told. Not that it really mattered, in any case. She wasn't interested in men. There were times when she wondered if she ever would be again. But that just wasn't an issue now. She had far more important things on her mind. . . .

Her thoughts broke off abruptly as the man called Gévaudan turned. There was the briefest hush again, almost imperceptible; if Joey hadn't been so focused on him and what had happened, she might never have noticed. For the first time she could see him clearly as he stepped into the light.

The first impression was of power. It was as if she could see some kind of aura around the man—too strong a feeling to dismiss, as much as it went against the grain. Within a moment Joey had an instinctive grasp of why this Luke Gévaudan had such a peculiar effect on the townspeople. He seemed to be having a similar effect on her.

Her eyes slid up his lithe form, from the commonplace boots and over the snug, faded jeans that molded long, muscular legs. She skipped quickly over his midtorso and took in the expanse of chest and broad shoulders, enhanced rather than hidden by the deep green plaid of his shirt. But it was when she reached his face that the full force of that first impression hit her.

He couldn't have been called handsome—not in

that yuppified modern style represented by the clean-cut models in the ads back home. There was a roughness about him, but not quite the same unpolished coarseness that typified many of the local men. Instead, there was a difference—a uniqueness—that she couldn't quite compare to anyone she'd seen before.

Her unwillingly fascinated gaze traveled over the strong, sharply cut lines of his jaw, along lips that held a hint of reserved mobility in their stillness. His nose was straight and even, the cheekbones high and hard, hollowed underneath with shadow. The hair that fell in tousled shocks over his forehead was mainly dark but liberally shot with gray, especially at the temples. The age this might have suggested was visible nowhere in his face or body, though his bearing announced experience. His stance was lightly poised, alert, almost coiled, like some wary creature from the wilds.

But it wasn't until she reached his eyes that it all coalesced into comprehension. They glowed. She shook her head, not sure what she was seeing. It wasn't a literal glow, she reminded herself with a last grasp at logic, but those eyes shone with their own inner light. They burned—they burned on hers. Her breath caught in her throat. He was staring at her, and for the first time she realized he was returning her examination.

She met his gaze unflinchingly for a long moment. His eyes were pale—and though in the dim light she could not make out the color, she could sense the warm light of amber in their depths. Striking, unusual eyes. Eyes that burned. Eyes that seemed never to blink but held hers in an unnerving, viselike grip. Eyes that seemed hauntingly familiar. . . .

Joey realized she was shaking when she finally

looked away. Her hands were clasped together in her lap, straining against each other with an internal struggle she was suddenly conscious of. Even now she could feel his gaze on her, intense and unwavering, but she resisted the urge to look up and meet it again. The loss of control she'd felt in those brief, endless moments of contact had been as unexpected and frightening as it was inexplicable. She wasn't eager to repeat the experience. But the small, stubborn core of her that demanded control over herself and her surroundings pricked at her without mercy. With a soft curse on an indrawn breath, Joey looked up.

He was gone.

Some secrets are too seductive to keep, and
too dangerous to reveal.

WHISPERED LIES
by
Christy Cohen

*For thirty-seven years Leah Shaperson had been trapped in
a marriage devoid of passion. Then a stranger's tanta-
lizing touch awakened her desires, and she found that she'd
do anything to feel wanted once more . . . even submit to
reckless games and her lover's darkest fantasies. But she
would soon learn that the price of forbidden pleasure is
steep. . . .*

"I know," Elliot said. His voice was hoarse and the
words were garbled.

"What?"

"I said I know," Elliot said, turning to her. He
showed her a face she didn't recognize, red with suppressed rage. She clutched her nightgown to her
chest.

"You know what?" she asked. She would make
him say it. She still could not believe he knew. No
one could know and not say anything. He had come
home on time tonight and they'd had dinner together. How could he sit through a whole dinner with
her and not say anything? How could he have sat
through so many dinners, gotten through so many
days, and still kept quiet?

Elliot stepped toward her, his face and neck blistering from rage, and Leah saw James's face in his.
She saw the recklessness, the fury, the need to lash

out. She stepped back, but then Elliot turned from her and lunged for the bed. He yanked the blankets off and threw them on the floor. Then he grabbed the pillows, flung them hard against the mattress, then hurled them across the room. He stared back at her, burned her with his gaze, then, in one viciously graceful move, swiped his arm across the dresser, knocking over frames and bottles of perfume. Glass shattered on the hardwood floor and liquid seeped into the wood, bombarding the room with fragrances.

Elliot looked around wildly. He started toward her and Leah jumped back, but then he turned and ran to the closet. He flung open the door and grabbed one of Leah's blouses. He ripped it off the hanger, then hurled it at her face.

Leah watched this man, this alien man, as he ripped off blouse after blouse and flung each one at her harder than the one before. She did not back away when the clothes hit her. She took every shot, was somehow relieved at the stinging on her cheeks, as if, after all, she was getting what she'd always thought she deserved.

She stood in silence, in awe, in dreamlike fear. Elliot went through the entire closet, ripped out every piece of her clothing. When he was through, he picked up her shoes and sailed them right for her head. Leah screamed and ducked and then, for the first time, understood that he hated her and ran out of the room.

He was faster and he grabbed her before she could get to the bathroom to lock herself inside. He pulled her into the kitchen, flipped on the glaring fluorescent lights, and fixed her with a stare that chilled her.

"I know you've been seeing James Arlington for three years," he said, the words straight and precise as arrows. "I know you've gone to him every Tuesday and Thursday night and screwed his brains out in his office. I know you went to him the day we got home from the cabin."

Leah slumped, and as if every word were a fist pounding on her head, she fell toward the floor. By the time he was through, she was down on her knees, crying. He stared at her, seemed to finally see her through his fury, and then pushed her away in disgust. She had to brace herself to keep from crashing into the kitchen cabinets.

"I've always known!" Elliot shouted. "You thought I was a fool, that I'd stopped looking at you. But I was always looking. Always!"

"So why didn't you do anything?" Leah shouted back up at him.

His eyes were wide, frenzied, and Leah pulled herself up. She backed into the corner of the kitchen.

"Because I loved you," he said, his anger turning to pain. He started crying, miming sounds with his mouth. Leah was both repulsed and drawn to him. She didn't know a thing about him, she realized in that instant. She had not known he was capable of shouting, of going crazy, of ransacking their bedroom. She had not known he could feel so much pain, that he must have been feeling it all along.

"Because," he went on when he could, "I thought it would pass. I thought you'd come back to me."

"I never left you," Leah said.

Elliot's head jerked up and his tears stopped abruptly. The knives sat on the counter by his hand and he pulled out a steak knife. Leah's eyes widened as he fingered the blade.

"You think I'm crazy," he said. "You think I'd hurt you."

"I don't know what to think."

He stepped toward her, smiling, the knife still in his hand. She raised her hand to her mouth, and then Elliot quickly turned and threw the knife across the room like a carnival performer. It landed in the sofa and stuck out like an extremity.

"I saw him open the door to you," Elliot said, grabbing her arm. "His fancy silk robe was hanging open. I could see him from the road. I kept thinking, 'She won't walk in. Leah would be sickened by a display like that.' But you weren't. You were eating it up."

"He makes me feel things!" Leah shouted. She was the one who was crying now. "He wants me. He's excited by me. You can't even—"

They stared at each other and, for a moment, Elliot came back to her. His face crumbled, the anger disintegrated, and she saw him, her husband. She touched his cheek.

"Oh, El, we've got to stop this."

He jerked away at her touch and stood up straight. He turned around and walked back to the bedroom. He looked at the mess in confusion, as if he couldn't remember what he had done. Then he walked to the closet, pulled out the suitcase, and opened it up on the bed.

Leah came in and stood by the door. She thought, *I'm dreaming. If anyone's going to leave, it will be me.* But as she thought this, Elliot packed his underwear and socks and shirts and pants in his suitcase and then snapped it shut.

He walked past her without a word. He set the suitcase down by the front door and then walked into the dining room. He took his briefcase off the table and walked out the door.

And don't miss these heart-stopping
romances from Bantam Books,
on sale in September:

THIEF OF HEARTS
by the nationally bestselling author

Teresa Medeiros

"Teresa Medeiros writes rare love stories
to cherish."
—*Romantic Times*

COURTING MISS HATTIE
by the highly acclaimed

Pamela Morsi

"A refreshing new voice in romance."
—*New York Times* bestselling author Jude Deveraux

VIRGIN BRIDE
by the sensational

Tamara Leigh

"Tamara Leigh writes fresh, exciting and
wonderfully sensual historical romance."
—*New York Times* bestselling author Amanda Quick

OFFICIAL RULES

To enter the sweepstakes below carefully follow all instructions found elsewhere in this offer.

The **Winners Classic** will award prizes with the following approximate maximum values: 1 Grand Prize: $26,500 (or $25,000 cash alternate); 1 First Prize: $3,000; 5 Second Prizes: $400 each; 35 Third Prizes: $100 each; 1,000 Fourth Prizes: $7.50 each. Total maximum retail value of Winners Classic Sweepstakes is $42,500. Some presentations of this sweepstakes may contain individual entry numbers corresponding to one or more of the aforementioned prize levels. To determine the Winners, individual entry numbers will first be compared with the winning numbers preselected by computer. For winning numbers not returned, prizes will be awarded in random drawings from among all eligible entries received. Prize choices may be offered at various levels. If a winner chooses an automobile prize, all license and registration fees, taxes, destination charges and, other expenses not offered herein are the responsibility of the winner. If a winner chooses a trip, travel must be complete within one year from the time the prize is awarded. Minors must be accompanied by an adult. Travel companion(s) must also sign release of liability. Trips are subject to space and departure availability. Certain black-out dates may apply.

The following applies to the sweepstakes named above:

No purchase necessary. You can also enter the sweepstakes by sending your name and address to: P.O. Box 508, Gibbstown, N.J. 08027. Mail each entry separately. Sweepstakes begins 6/1/93. Entries must be received by 12/30/94. Not responsible for lost, late, damaged, misdirected, illegible or postage due mail. Mechanically reproduced entries are not eligible. All entries become property of the sponsor and will not be returned.

Prize Selection/Validations: Selection of winners will be conducted no later than 5:00 PM on January 28, 1995, by an independent judging organization whose decisions are final. Random drawings will be held at 1211 Avenue of the Americas, New York, N.Y. 10036. Entrants need not be present to win. Odds of winning are determined by total number of entries received. Circulation of this sweepstakes is estimated not to exceed 200 million. All prizes are guaranteed to be awarded and delivered to winners. Winners will be notified by mail and may be required to complete an affidavit of eligibility and release of liability which must be returned within 14 days of date on notification or alternate winners will be selected in a random drawing. Any prize notification letter or any prize returned to a participating sponsor, Bantam Doubleday Dell Publishing Group, Inc., its participating divisions or subsidiaries, or the independent judging organization as undeliverable will be awarded to an alternate winner. Prizes are not transferable. No substitution for prizes except as offered or as may be necessary due to unavailability, in which case a prize of equal or greater value will be awarded. Prizes will be awarded approximately 90 days after the drawing. All taxes are the sole responsibility of the winners. Entry constitutes permission (except where prohibited by law) to use winners' names, hometowns, and likenesses for publicity purposes without further or other compensation. Prizes won by minors will be awarded in the name of parent or legal guardian.

Participation: Sweepstakes open to residents of the United States and Canada, except for the province of Quebec. Sweepstakes sponsored by Bantam Doubleday Dell Publishing Group, Inc., (BDD), 1540 Broadway, New York, NY 10036. Versions of this sweepstakes with different graphics and prize choices will be offered in conjunction with various solicitations or promotions by different subsidiaries and divisions of BDD. Where applicable, winners will have their choice of any prize offered at level won. Employees of BDD, its divisions, subsidiaries, advertising agencies, independent judging organization, and their immediate family members are not eligible.

Canadian residents, in order to win, must first correctly answer a time limited arithmetical skill testing question. Void in Puerto Rico, Quebec and wherever prohibited or restricted by law. Subject to all federal, state, local and provincial laws and regulations. For a list of major prize winners (available after 1/29/95): send a self-addressed, stamped envelope entirely separate from your entry to: Sweepstakes Winners, P.O. Box 517, Gibbstown, NJ 08027. Requests must be received by 12/30/94. DO NOT SEND ANY OTHER CORRESPONDENCE TO THIS P.O. BOX.

Don't miss these fabulous Bantam women's fiction titles

On Sale in September

THIEF OF HEARTS

by **Teresa Medeiros**, bestselling author of *A Whisper of Roses*

"Ms. Medeiros casts a spell with her poignant writing."
—*Rendezvous*

From the storm-lashed decks of a pirate schooner to the elegant grounds of an English estate comes a spellbinding tale of love and deception as only the remarkable Teresa Medeiros can tell it.
❏ *56332-7 $5.50/6.99 in Canada*

COURTING MISS HATTIE

by **Pamela Morsi**, bestselling author of *Wild Oats*

"A refreshing new voice in romance."—Jude Deveraux

Pamela Morsi has won readers' hearts with her unforgettable novels—filled with romance, humor, and her trademark down-to-earth charm. And with *Courting Miss Hattie*, Morsi pairs an unlikely bride and an irresistible suitor who learn that love can be found in the most unlikely places.
❏ *29000-2 $5.50/6.99 in Canada*

VIRGIN BRIDE

by **Tamara Leigh**

"Fresh, exciting...wonderfully sensual...sure to be noticed in the romance genre."—Amanda Quick

Tamara Leigh burst onto the romance scene with *Warrior Bride* and was praised by authors and critics alike. Now with *Virgin Bride,* she offers another electrifying tale of a woman who would give anything to avoid being sent to a convent—even her virtue.
❏ *56536-2 $5.50/6.99 in Canada*

Bestselling Women's Fiction

Sandra Brown

28951-9	TEXAS! LUCKY	$5.99/6.99 in Canada
28990-X	TEXAS! CHASE	$5.99/6.99
29500-4	TEXAS! SAGE	$5.99/6.99
29085-1	22 INDIGO PLACE	$5.99/6.99
29783-X	A WHOLE NEW LIGHT	$5.99/6.99
56045-X	TEMPERATURES RISING	$5.99/6.99
56274-6	FANTA C	$4.99/5.99
56278-9	LONG TIME COMING	$4.99/5.99

Amanda Quick

28354-5	SEDUCTION	$5.99/6.99
28932-2	SCANDAL	$5.99/6.99
28594-7	SURRENDER	$5.99/6.99
29325-7	RENDEZVOUS	$5.99/6.99
29316-8	RECKLESS	$5.99/6.99
29316-8	RAVISHED	$4.99/5.99
29317-6	DANGEROUS	$5.99/6.99
56506-0	DECEPTION	$5.99/7.50

Nora Roberts

29078-9	GENUINE LIES	$5.99/6.99
28578-5	PUBLIC SECRETS	$5.99/6.99
26461-3	HOT ICE	$5.99/6.99
26574-1	SACRED SINS	$5.99/6.99
27859-2	SWEET REVENGE	$5.99/6.99
27283-7	BRAZEN VIRTUE	$5.99/6.99
29597-7	CARNAL INNOCENCE	$5.50/6.50
29490-3	DIVINE EVIL	$5.99/6.99

Iris Johansen

29871-2	LAST BRIDGE HOME	$4.50/5.50
29604-3	THE GOLDEN BARBARIAN	$4.99/5.99
29244-7	REAP THE WIND	$4.99/5.99
29032-0	STORM WINDS	$4.99/5.99
28855-5	THE WIND DANCER	$4.95/5.95
29968-9	THE TIGER PRINCE	$5.50/6.50
29944-1	THE MAGNIFICENT ROGUE	$5.99/6.99
29945-X	BELOVED SCOUNDREL	$5.99/6.99

Ask for these titles at your bookstore or use this page to order.

Please send me the books I have checked above. I am enclosing $_____ (add $2.50 to cover postage and handling). Send check or money order, no cash or C.O.D.'s please.

Mr./ Ms. _____

Address _____

City/ State/ Zip _____

Send order to: Bantam Books, Dept. FN 16, 2451 S. Wolf Road, Des Plaines, IL 60018

Please allow four to six weeks for delivery.

Prices and availability subject to change without notice.   FN 16 - 4/94